THROUGH GLASS EYES

THE AUTOBIOGRAPHY OF A 1975
TRIUMPH DOLOMITE SPRINT

THROUGH GLASS EYES

THE AUTOBIOGRAPHY OF A 1975 TRIUMPH DOLOMITE SPRINT

Paul Chiswick

ATHENA PRESS
LONDON

THROUGH GLASS EYES
The Autobiography of a 1975
Triumph Dolomite Sprint
Copyright © Paul Chiswick 2009

ISBN 978 1 84748 486 4

First published 2009 by
ATHENA PRESS
Queen's House, 2 Holly Road
Twickenham TW1 4EG
United Kingdom

Printed for Athena Press

To Julie and Charlotte, the headlights of my life

Contents

The Silver Ones

The life-changing day I'd been dreading finally arrived. I'd hoped they might have had a change of heart before now. After all, it was in their power to reconsider such a thoughtless decision. If it had been possible, I would have got down on my bended knees and pleaded with them, 'Don't do this to me, please. Don't.'

But I don't have any knees.

They caught me entirely by surprise. No telltale signs, no convoluted clues, no tantalising giveaways. An 'on the spur of the moment' conclusion reached over breakfast one sultry Saturday morning was all it took to seal my fate. Since finding out, my sleep had been tortured by a dark and menacing presence that wouldn't leave it in peace. To think the final curtain was coming down on a performance that had amused, entertained, frustrated and delighted its actors in equal measures for the best part of thirty years. I shivered as my imagination toyed with the uncertain future they were pushing me into.

But let's not run before we can walk. There are events that need to be unwound, combed out neatly and rewound before I make my next, unasked-for journey.

August this year was wonderful again. In these feverish times it's arguably the only month that truly offers any relief from the hectic and hurried rush of new millennium life. School runs are slid into limbo for the duration, neighbourhoods are hushed as their residents pack their bags and jet off on bargain holidays abroad, and the few factories that are still left standing in this part of the country temporarily close for their annual shutdown. Leaves are slowly but steadily changing from a flecked palette of greens to the shimmering golds, browns and russets of autumn, and the air is sharp with the city tang trapped in the sequinned dews of early morning. This is the only time of year that you'll find the road menders noticeably absent. They too, have more pressing arrangements with the clamorous bars and beaches calling out to them from Spain and the Greek Islands, like irresistible sirens to forlorn, bewitched seamen. August is manna from heaven.

No. Better.

Normally at this early time of morning the uncomplaining main roads would be at their most laboured, their brawny backs rippling with the weight of the inconsiderate traffic rolling up and down them. The skinnier feeder roads are almost at breaking point, supporting an endless stream of crawling vehicles, multi-coloured dots in a choreographed workday pattern. Relief for them comes when the dots at long last spill out on to the muscular arterial roads where, like sprinters racing to the finishing line, they are accelerated to a speed which might get the drivers to their destinations if not on time then tolerably late.

It was now my turn to say goodbye to the feeder and partner the bypass in our ritual dance. My old engine began to rev higher as I cautiously pulled out and gathered speed as quickly as I could on the bypass.

Not quickly enough for some.

'Parp… parp… parp! Out of the way, old man! I'm in one helluva hurry! Parp… parp… parp! Move over!'

A stolen glance behind me bore out my suspicions. Well, well, what a surprise! I might have guessed it would be a silver one. Nowadays it nearly always is. They seem to be everywhere. Silver is the in colour, the first choice of professional footballers, minor celebrities and the newly minted. High on flash, low on taste.

'Come on… come on… MOVE OVER!' he screamed as he closed to within inches of my rear end.

I tut-tutted and concentrated hard as the man inside me gently and carefully coaxed me closer to the litter-strewn verge of the bypass. Nowadays it takes me some time to manoeuvre as the reflexes aren't what they were, and I'm much more aware of the dangers that lurk along the kerbside for the unsuspecting. Time and experience has taught me that a belief in immortality is only for the young and the foolish.

'About bloody time! Why don't you get yourself a collector!' the silver one spat at me as he flew by, far in excess of the designated speed limit.

There is definitely something about the silver ones I've grown to dislike. My lights don't focus as sharply as they once did – and I sometimes get confused in watery daylight or bright sunshine. So on occasion the silver ones catch me unawares. When that happens I know their bad-mannered abuse won't be too long in coming.

'Move over, old man!'

'Get out of the way, old man!'

'Is there something the matter with you, old man?'

'You should be on the scrapheap, old man!'

'About time a collector took you, old man!'

There are now far too many silver ones on the roads for comfort. They are arrogant, self-centred, have no respect, and show a complete absence of good manners. Many red ones have a similar temperament, but you don't see so many of them nowadays, and they were never as offensive as the silver ones. Some say they have nigh on eradicated the red ones, just as the more aggressive grey squirrel bullied its smaller cousin the red squirrel into obscurity.

Of course, it may be that nearly all the silver ones are foreign makes, whereas I'm a British thoroughbred, and arguably we've a more even-keeled temperament. You won't hear us honking our horns at the slightest excuse. That would be quite inappropriate behaviour. (Sometimes I wonder why the designers even gave us horns.) Not so the foreign makes – they revel in using their horns all the time. Mind you, they dominate the roads now and we British are in a tiny minority. Many speak English well, sometimes very well. Although that's not surprising as many of the foreign makes are made in Britain and they hear English from the day they're first screwed together. Though one must never, ever, refer to them as 'foreign makes'. Oh, no, there are severe laws to punish you if you do that! As far as they're concerned they are every bit as British as I am. They even consider themselves superior to their relatives who are assembled abroad and shipped to Britain. Would you believe that?

'I bet he's a sales rep,' remarked Roger dryly as he gently eased me away from the beckoning kerb. (Roger Bunting is my driver, and you'll be getting to know him much better later on.)

'Does it matter, darling? Just concentrate on your driving. We don't want to have an accident, particularly today, do we?' soothed Roger's perennial passenger, his wife, Sylvia.

Her words made me shudder.

Particularly today.

It's no secret that I'm past my prime. I may be almost thirty years of age but there are still a few miles left in this old dog yet. I'll possibly still be around when many of today's youngsters have burned themselves out, such is the pace at which they lead their lives and the thoughtless way they're treated by the drivers.

It wasn't like this back in the old days. Drivers used to be so courteous to each other. And they clearly thought much more of us cars, too. It wasn't unusual for a driver to own and care for a car for ten years or sometimes more. That began to change partly with the introduction of the cursed MOT test, as many drivers decided that rather than suffer the indignity of failing the MOT they would simply sell us to another driver and hand off this time-consuming and risky affair. In some cases even those drivers didn't want to be bothered with the next MOT (an annually occurring event) and so we started to be passed on, like an unwanted baton in a never-ending relay race.

The state of affairs was bad enough owing to the MOT, but it became a whole lot worse when the marketing men muscled in on the scene. They transformed us from being merely functional to being desirably fashionable. Sure, it wasn't all the marketing men's fault. We, like the drivers, were victims of our own fragile egos, and the marketing men had the tools and the knowledge to wrap the drivers and us round their collective little fingers. And wrap they did.

Thanks to the marketing men it wasn't very long before we were seen everywhere in glorious living colour   on television, in papers and magazines, pasted on billboards, even on the back of the buses (and how the dreary buses delighted in the unexpected attention they receive). The drivers became so mesmerised by all the marketing it was astonishing. Instead of simply being a convenient way to get from A to B, we cars were unstoppably and irreversibly propelled into the realm of status symbol, thanks to the manipulative messages of the marketing men. Every picture had a strap line, sometimes subtle, sometimes smacking of innuendo. All focused on the driver's Achilles heel – his ego. (I say 'his' because, remarkably, the few female drivers at that time were immune to the marketing men. No matter what tricks they tried on the female drivers it was about as effective as sawing away at an ancient oak with a nail file.)

Here are some fine examples of the marketing men at their very best:

'You can do it in an MG.'

'Style. It's hard to define but easy to recognise.'

'Big car. Small price.'

'The ultimate driving machine!'

'Grace, space, pace!'

The drivers just couldn't resist.

As pernicious as it was, not even the pairing of the MOT and the marketing men could persuade the drivers to part with their money on much less than a five-year cycle. It took one more ingredient in the heady cocktail to give the drivers a high: the annual number plate change.

This little sleight of hand was one of the greatest tricks ever played on the drivers by the British Government, with the tacit support of the makers. A little history would help to understand why this catalyst was so important in the lethal brew.

Number plates first appeared in Britain in 1904, five years after the Dutch authorities introduced the idea to the world. The first mark to be issued in London was the simple, bold A1, registered to Earl Russell. Cars then were a rare sight.

As the number of cars increased, number plates were made up from a local council identifier code of up to three letters (designating their area), followed by a random number, e.g. ABC 123. In the early 1950s, as numbers started to run out, the components were reversed, giving rise to registrations in the format 123 ABC. This style of registration survived for an incredible sixty years, until 1963, and there was nothing at all to indicate the year of issue. So you see, without knowledge of a particular maker's vehicles no one could determine with certainty the exact age of a car. In truth, no one really cared how old your car was. You were fortunate to have one.

By 1963 a number of local councils had run out of registrations. It was at this point that the Government performed the trick. They introduced the 'suffix system', a letter indicating the year of registration being added at the end of the plate. Thus 1963 plates had the format AAA 111A, 1964 plates AAA 111B, 1965 plates AAA 111C and so on. So now it was possible to determine precisely the age of a car and another social differentiator was created.

With the boom in the car population even this system survived only until 1983 when the 'classic prefix system' was introduced, with a single letter identifying the year of issue at the beginning of the registration mark. Thus, 1983 plates had the format A123 ABC, 1984 plates B123 ABC, 1985 plates D123 ABC and so on. This system continued until the end of August 2001, when it was necessary to change the system yet again with a new plate being introduced every six months!

The scene was set for a very expensive and wasteful new game – I Must Have a Car with the Latest Registration Plate.

Now the marketing men and the makers were in heaven.

They had trapped the drivers in a money-spinning treadmill.

'Particularly today.'

Sylvia's words came back to me.

What was going to happen today? Was this to be the day I had been terrified of? I kept asking myself how I could have displeased them. Was it the trouble we had two summers ago when I'd suffered that embarrassing breakdown? Or last winter when it was so cold I just couldn't start in the mornings?

I tried in vain to work out their logic. In my naivety I never dreamt that the status quo we'd known for so long wouldn't continue indefinitely. That's what happens when you follow a habit day in, day out, year in, year out. Complacency sets in and it's damned difficult to do away with it.

There were so many memories. Thirty years of shared experiences. Three decades of a colourful journey through interwoven lives. How could they do this to me? What in heaven's name had I done to deserve this? The relationship between us had been closer than a marriage. I had been parent and child to them at the same time. This felt like the ultimate rejection.

Roger and Sylvia had decided to sell me.

My Driver and his Wife

Roger Peter Bunting is an only child. His father, Alan, worked as a gardener for a small local municipality the entire duration of his working life. A reserved, unassuming and introspective man, Alan went about his business without much ambition beyond the day-to-day duties of his job. He was a home bird, often to be found enjoying carpentry activities in a creaky, shiplap shed at the bottom of his garden, was seldom seen in the local pub, and was in many ways an unremarkable citizen.

But Alan had a dark passion. He was a closet Hell's Angel.

It had started in Alan's early teens. Alan's eldest brother, Alf, had spent several years in America as a hired hand after demobbing from the Parachute Regiment. While working on a cattle ranch in Utah, Alf stumbled upon a local chapter of the Hell's Angels. Being a larger-than-life character, he'd fallen in with the chapter on account of his addiction to the adrenaline rush he'd missed since leaving the Paras. Alf also liked the unsavoury reputation that the Angels enjoyed (although in time he came to realise that this was perception rather than reality), and took pleasure in being part of a close brotherhood, something he'd had in his military years. He also fancied the blowsy girls that hung around with the Angels, and had taken up with and married a busty, five-foot-nothing blonde hellcat called Gloria. They lived happily in a small, clapboard house in Bluffdale for a number of years until Gloria, out of the blue one day, announced to Alf that it was about time they thought about having children. Unfortunately for her, kids were not in Alf's life plan, and he told Gloria so in no uncertain terms. Gloria shrugged, said nothing and simply shook her luxuriant, lacquered curls from side to side. The very next day he had an unexpected visit from the entire chapter. Their ultimatum was final – he wasn't welcome in the group and it wouldn't be wise for Alf to remain in their town in future. As tough a nut as he was, Alf took the wise course and departed. He never heard anything further from Gloria and he never rode with any Angels again. Word travels fast and it travels far.

Periodically, Alf sent letters back to his brother in England graphically describing his time with the Angels – not without embellishment it may be said. The young Alan lapped up the stories, especially the vivid descriptions of the customised Harleys and Indians and the colourful and larger-than-life characters such as 'Redhat' Hank and 'Skunk' Cheroot who rode them on the dusty desert roads of Utah. He envied Alf's carefree life, and imagined himself the leader of a local chapter, replete with tasselled leathers and a booming, multicoloured chopper. It was a dream he was determined to make reality.

When, in his mid twenties, he was able to afford a decent bike – and one which was acceptable to the Angels – he joined a local chapter and was given the nickname 'Pruner' on account of his horticultural skills. For the next fifteen years Pruner rode with his chapter all over the UK, raising eyebrows and receiving fearful looks wherever they went. No one knew that really they were just a bunch of ordinary guys who liked to dress in worn, black leather and ride big, slow and noisy motorbikes. There were engineers, accountants, lawyers and even one professional footballer in the chapter. Who else could afford to join a HOG?

In his late twenties, while on a week-long ride, Alan met Irene, the receptionist in a small hotel in Derbyshire. Irene's hotel was tolerant of Angels and its pastoral setting became a regular meeting place for the growing number of chapters spreading throughout the country at that time. It wasn't exactly love at first sight, but the tall, willowy Alan and the quiet, sandy-haired Irene spent the week chatting to each other in the hotel bar long after she had finished her shift. At the end of the week they agreed to meet again soon.

It was the beginning of a courtship that was to last almost a decade, with Alan regularly commuting from his small cottage in the South West of England to Irene's parents' home nestled among the rounded hills and gritstone escarpments of the Peak District. Finally, on Alan's thirty-eighth birthday, he popped the question, and six months later they were married in a small church in a village just outside Barchester, and the Derbyshire lass took up residence in her new husband's home 'down south'. Within two months of marrying she found herself pregnant with Roger, who was to be their one and only child.

Alan never gave up riding with the Angels. In 1978, two days after his birthday, he dropped dead from a massive heart attack while on a ride. He was seventy-one years old.

The young Roger was very like his father in many ways. A lanky, quiet and intense boy he journeyed through a largely uneventful early childhood, the highlight of which was, to the delight of his parents, passing his eleven plus and thus gaining entrance to the prestigious Barchester Boys Grammar School. During his time there he neither excelled academically nor at sports, but he was well-liked and as he got older shed some of the reserve of his earlier childhood. He took part in the usual teenage male hobbies, involved in turn with fishing, cycling, war-gaming, and finally ending up as one of the school's whizz-kids in the fledgling chess club. There was never any contact with girls; the school was single sex and his circle had absolutely no interest in parties, discos or pubs – pursuits eagerly indulged in by most young people of his age.

By the time Roger reached the upper sixth a revolution was taking place focused on the dying port of Liverpool. A group of four young local musicians was breaking all conventions and creating an unstoppable spread of teenage mania throughout the country which was later to cross the water to America. The uprising simply passed Roger and his friends by, engrossed as they were in Larsen's Opening and the complex intricacies of Dutch, Sicilian and Grunfeld's Defences. The Beatles might as well have been Venusians.

Not unexpectedly, he failed his A levels by quite a margin, thus missing out on any opportunity to go to university, which was the single ambition of many grammar school pupils. If his parents were displeased they didn't show it. It was as if Alan and Irene were content their child had achieved more than they had by getting to grammar school. Besides, it wasn't as bad as it first seemed as only some three per cent of school leavers achieved a university placement then.

Academic failure didn't come as a disappointment to Roger.

He had his heart set on owning a Lambretta. What he did need was a job so he could save money to buy the scooter.

Alas, Roger seemed clueless as to how he was going to earn a living. The young man had absolutely no idea of what kind of career he wanted, and passed the next two years muddling around in a variety of mundane jobs – cleaning windows, working in a butcher's shop, labouring for a chain-smoking bricklayer, and finally dressing mannequins in the Barchester branch of a major clothing chain. At the end of it he still didn't have enough money for the Lambretta.

It was Uncle Alf who rescued the rudderless youth.

Thanks to his outgoing and effusive nature (which had mellowed in recent years), Uncle Alf had been invited to join one of Barchester's Masonic lodges where he quickly became popular owing to his bottomless pit of army stories and Hell's Angel anecdotes. One of the advantages of being in the lodge was that Alf got to make friends with many influential local businessmen, and often helped to 'sort out their problems' when they ran into difficulties of a, shall we say, delicate nature. Alf thus established himself as the 'fixer' in the lodge, and in this capacity stored up quite a stock of favours owed him over the years. It was one of these favours he called in for Roger – and got him a position as a trainee accountant with a small but thriving local practice.

In a remarkably short time Roger discovered he had a previously undiscovered talent for accountancy. He revelled in working with figures and devoured the many accounting rules and codes that were in constant flux. Everything he could read on accountancy he did, volunteering for any mundane accounting task, and attending night school courses to supplement his daytime experience. Within two years he had become a subject expert on the treatment of small business accounts and was highly regarded by the partners in the practice. Passing his professional examinations with flying colours he was well set for an associate position, given time. Then for reasons that he never explained satisfactorily to either his parents or Uncle Alf, he decided he'd outgrown his employer and needed to move on. So he applied for, and obtained, a position in the Charities Division of a much larger firm in the same town.

It was here that his upward rise in the profession plateaued, a situation with which Roger Peter Bunting seemed quite contented.

He never bought the Lambretta.

Sylvia Margaret Bunting (nee Urquhart) is a different kettle of fish altogether. The eldest of three daughters, Sylvia comes from a very privileged background. Her paternal grandfather started a fine-furniture-making business shortly before the First World War, and through a combination of hard work, dogged sales-manship and shrewd investment grew it to be one of the country's most recognisable brands by the late forties.

On his death in 1953 after a protracted illness, his only son Reginald took over the mantle from the old man, and saw an opportunity to get into the lucrative Western European market and compete with the French and the Italians, which he did extremely effectively with the substantial backing of the British Government during one of its many export drives. Business boomed and the family became seriously wealthy, moving to a sprawling mansion near to Kingston-upon-Thames. In 1956, when she was just five years old, Sylvia was sent as a boarder to the prestigious Adcote School for Girls in rural Shropshire where she was recognised by her teachers as 'a pupil who knows her own mind, and exactly what she wants'. It would appear the young girl had favoured the genes of her paternal grandfather.

In 1962 her parents transferred her to the even more expensive Roedean School in Brighton, where the young Sylvia flourished. She was extremely popular with both her teachers and her classmates, and had a talent for organisation coupled with an ability to work hard in order to succeed at whatever she turned her hand to. By the time she was in the lower sixth form she'd been captain of her year's hockey and netball teams, had chaired the school's debating society, and was pencilled in by her teachers as a prime candidate for the Oxbridge entrance examinations. The odds-on bet was that she would also make School Captain. Prospects were looking very good for Sylvia.

Then disaster struck.

Early one cold and mist-shrouded October morning, while she was at home for the half term holiday, she was awoken from her slumbers by the sound of a car crunching to a halt on the gravel drive below her bedroom window. Gently opening a crack in the curtains and peeping through, she could see a large, black Jaguar with the driver's door and boot wide open on the sweeping crescent below. Seconds later there was a frantic banging on the front door followed by a creaking as the heavy door was pulled open. There followed a rapid exchange of voices, one of which she recognised as her father's. She'd hardly slipped on her dressing gown, which was hanging behind her bedroom door, when the front door slammed shut. Rushing back to the window she looked out just in time to see her father heave a suitcase into the Jaguar's boot, quickly slide into the passenger seat, and slam the car door shut. It then shot off at high speed, spewing cream-coloured stones all over the diamanté dew that twinkled on the clipped lawn.

She didn't see her father again that day. Nor the next day. Nor the following week. In fact, she never saw her father again. Ever.

She wasn't the only one who never saw him again, though there were many who desperately wanted to. Those who most desired an audience with Reginald Urquhart, Chairman and Managing Director of The Imperial Fine Furniture Company Limited, were his creditors and Her Majesty's Inland Revenue.

It transpired that the king of fine furniture hadn't exactly been open and honest with his bankers, lawyers, auditors, business associates, suppliers, customers, and (unforgivably) Her Majesty's Government. No, that would be putting it too mildly. Reginald was a crook. A very clever crook, but a crook all the same. Unfortunately for him he'd been found out by one of his female accounting staff who had uncovered several interesting anomalies in the books. This may have gone unreported had not the person in question been sexually approached by the philandering Reginald, and then dismissed on account of not welcoming his suggestive advances. The woman, in a fit of pique, then told her policeman brother, who not surprisingly dutifully reported it to the appropriate authorities.

As luck would have it, Reginald was forewarned by a jealous colleague of the sacked woman and had taken the only course he felt was available to him. He skipped.

If his creditors couldn't have Reginald, they resolved to have anything they could from his family. And they did. The family was left with little apart from the clothes they wore and a few personal effects.

The result was calamitous. Within weeks, Sylvia's beleaguered mother suffered a nervous breakdown. Her mother's eldest sister, Mavis, a GP in the West Country town of Barchester, was informed and came to look after her stricken sister. Aunt Mavis was unmarried and regarded as the matron of the family. Whenever there was a problem Aunt Mavis was the one to bear it on her shoulders and sort it out. She'd entered the medical profession against the wishes of her father, Sylvia's maternal grandfather, who had objected on the grounds that it would take too much out of her personal life. He was right. Aunt Mavis's dedication to her patients in the community in which she lived left little time for forming relationships or meeting people apart from her professional colleagues and patients. She hadn't had any opportunity to stumble across someone she might spend her life with, and had thus remained single and childless. Now she was a rather serious fifty-six-year-old, with a well-deserved retirement planned in four years' time.

Aunt Mavis knew she might now have to delay her anticipated retirement and help her sister and her young family. It would have been beneficial if she could call on June for assistance, but she knew June only too well.

Ah, June. The black sheep of the family. June was Mavis's younger sister. She was always the one who could bend her father round her little finger; always the one who created any excuse to avoid chores at home; always the one who got Mavis to do her homework for her; always the one who argued and upset her mother; always the one who had far more interest in boys than she should have had. At seventeen she ran away with a heavily tattooed fairground worker and vanished from sight. Her parents were distraught. Three months later she coolly reappeared and announced to the world that she was going to work as a secretary in London, that the fairground worker was a 'passing fancy', and there was to be no argument. Which there was of course, but all to no avail as June had her way again, as usual. She packed her case and caught the train to Paddington.

The family didn't hear from her much during the next two years. Then out of the blue one day they received an invitation to a wedding: June's wedding. She'd met and fallen in love with a New Zealander who worked for a large firm of consulting civil engineers in the City. The wedding was to be in April, and the invitation was concluded with: 'Oh by the way, Lance and I will be moving to New Zealand as he feels the opportunities there are better than those offered in the UK. I'll see you at the church. Love to all, June.'

In July the newly-weds set sail for New Zealand, never to return. But there was to be a sad turn of events for June. She found that Lance was incapable of giving her any children. To offset their disappointment they put their total energy into building his business, which by and by successfully acquired an enviable reputation on South Island. By the time Sylvia's father left his family in the lurch June and Lance were semi-retired, living on the fruits of their business's success and spending most of their time travelling to see exotic places. The last thing June wanted was to face up to any problems her extended family might have 'back in the old country'. June was June after all, and a leopard doesn't change its spots.

That left Aunt Mavis with some difficult choices, which she faced stoically. There was no way that she could leave three teenage nieces without a home, and for the immediate future she decided they would come to live with her in Barchester. Maintaining all three of them at public school was out of the question. They would have to transfer to local schools. Their mother's future would need to be considered more profoundly, given her delicate condition and fragile financial state.

Consequently, Sylvia never returned to Roedean. Instead she was sent to attend Barchester High School for Girls. Having barely six months to adjust to a new home and new school and distressed by the loss of her father and her mother's relapse, it was little wonder that she failed her A levels. The dream of a fine university education followed by a lucrative career went up in smoke. She moped around Aunt Mavis's house from July until December at which time Aunt Mavis took it upon herself to find a position for the girl. A good friend and patient, a certain Mr George Fleesem, was asked if he had any openings in his accountancy practice for 'an intelligent and trustworthy girl who needs to make a living'. Fleesem replied that he did indeed have an opening as one of his ladies had taken early retirement owing to ill health, and he would be only too pleased to interview Sylvia.

So on the third day of January in 1970 Sylvia Urquhart turned up for her first day of work in the Charities Division of Robsem, Fleesem and Crooks, Chartered Accountants.

'Roger, this is Miss Urquhart. She'll be helping us out now that Miss Molyneux has retired,' declared the dapper man in the dark blue pinstripe suit, gazing down over the top of his silver bifocals at the young man assiduously scribbling away in a notebook in front of him.

Roger sighed in frustration as his train of thought was broken. It was hard enough trying to unpick the tortuous and incomplete accounts of the British Myopia Foundation, without being interrupted to be introduced to a new member of staff. He glanced up and was engaged by the deepest green eyes he had ever seen, set in an unblemished face framed by a magnificent mane of wavy, auburn hair. Those eyes looked unblinkingly back at him and he felt as if they were gazing into his very soul.

'S… s… sorry, Mr Fleesem. I was miles away with the BMF's accounts.' He rose to his feet and held out his hand to the possessor of the green eyes. 'Roger. Roger Bunting. Pleased to meet you, Miss… er…'

'Urquhart, Roger. Miss Urquhart. She'll be working in Charities for the next six months,' interjected the pinstripe suit.

'It's a pleasure to meet you too, Mr Bunting. I'm looking forward to working with you all. Mr Fleesem tells me what a marvellous department this is.' Sylvia smiled sweetly at the elegant gentleman, who gave a little cough, blushed slightly and brushed an imaginary speck of dust off his lapel.

'Hmm, quite. Miss Urquhart will be assigned to Mrs Mellors. Please make her welcome, Roger. Come, Miss Urquhart, I'll introduce you to Mr Crooks in the Partners' Suite.' The pinstripe suit flapped his hand and off they went.

The impact of Sylvia Urquhart on the office was immediate. Most of the female staff of Robsem, Fleesem and Crooks were women well into their fifties and, with respect to the traditions of the accounting profession, dressed appropriately in uninspiring shades of muddy browns and cowshit greens. Sylvia broke the mould. She loved wearing the colour red, which set off her abundant auburn hair and her mesmeric green eyes. The effect she had on the predominantly male office was astonishing.

One Monday morning Trevor Blease, acknowledged by all as possibly the dullest individual in the firm if not the world, discarded his time-worn, shapeless, dark blue suit, crumpled, yellowish-white shirt, and nondescript, curry-stained tie in favour of a new, dark grey pinstripe suit, stylish button-down pale blue shirt and striped red silk tie. This was the signal for the start of an undeclared sartorial contest among all the males in the firm who came into contact with the magnificent Sylvia. It was finally brought to a climax one Thursday morning when David Dell-Bywater, old Harrovian and a safe bet for a future partner, turned up for work in a lightweight pale grey suit, pink shirt, saffron tie and shiny grey loafers. This was the straw that finally broke the camel's back. The hapless Dell-Bywater was publicly bollocked by Mr Robsem in the open office, told he was a disgrace to the firm, and ordered to go home and change into something more suited to his profession. Things rapidly returned to normal after that.

It wasn't only Sylvia's looks that were getting her noticed. Before long it became apparent that she was incredibly efficient at whatever task was set for her. She didn't shirk any chore, however mundane, and her amazing organising ability was highly regarded by the older women in the office who treated her more like a daughter than a colleague.

Visits to Charities from the Messrs Fleesem, Robsem and Crooks also became more frequent. They had previously been almost invisible in this, the least glamorous area of the partnership, yet hardly a day now passed without a visit from one or the other of the venerable gentlemen. It wasn't just the presence of the young lady who always wore red, either. There was now a new, positive mood in Charities that wasn't equalled in other areas of the firm. An atmosphere of teamwork, never previously known, had begun to take root. Lately, and also unprecedented, there had even been requests from other divisions for transfers into Charities.

Before long Sylvia became indispensable. If you wanted something doing quickly and proficiently, Sylvia was the person to do it. If you wanted to know where something was, Sylvia was the person to ask. Sylvia had all the answers. Sylvia got things done. Sylvia was here to stay.

The senior partner looked around at the crowd of faces in front of him. The Partners' Dining Room and anteroom were full to the brim with the firm's employees, invited in by the old man. Casting a rheumy eye over the multitude he felt his chest tighten as mixed emotions vied with each other. He clapped his hands and the room fell silent.

'Thank you all for coming. As you know, it's my seventy-fifth birthday today and after much deliberation I've come to the conclusion I'm well past my sell-by date.'

There was a nervous tittering.

'That being so, I would like to do something different with the years that are remaining to me. As you may know, my father was one of the two founding partners of this firm, and I was invited to join him as a young man when I graduated more than fifty years ago. At that time there were but five of us in the business and we did everything ourselves. I even remember my father attempting to type his own letters at one point – a skill he never mastered, I'm afraid. Anyway, from those humble beginnings Fleesem and Pinchett – as we were known in those days – has grown to be a 150-person practice operating out of six offices around the region. We've done well, and I'd like to thank you all for contributing to our success. I'm a very proud man.' Coughing nervously, he paused to take a sip of water from a tumbler that was placed on the table to the side of him.

He continued. 'But now, it's time for a change. I have decided after much soul-searching to retire with immediate effect. From the beginning of next month the firm will be run by Mr Robsem as senior partner, ably assisted by Mr Crooks. I can also reveal that there will be a full review of the number of junior partners and associates we have in the business, as it is agreed among the partners that we are rather light in that area.'

A murmur went up around the room at this news. It had been quite a while since promotions to the ranks of junior partner and associate had been made, and this had become a contentious, if not demoralising, issue within the firm.

Mr Fleesem added, 'We feel Charities have suffered most in this respect when compared to other divisions and there will be a number of announcements next week that will address this. I'd like to go out on a high and I feel this is probably the best way to do it. However, don't think you've seen the last of me – I shall return from time to time to make sure no unauthorised personnel are using the Partners' Cloakroom!'

Raucous laughter broke out at this, and a loud cheer went up. The old man felt his throat tighten and a glistening tear appeared in the corner of his eye. He coughed loudly once more and raised his hand. The gathering fell silent.

'Thank you, thank you. I wish you all the best in your individual and collective endeavours. Back to the grindstone now!'

Clapping burst out around the room as he shuffled through the mass of people, shaking hands with many of his staff for the last time.

'Do you think you'll get promoted?' whispered Sylvia to the tall young man squashed next to her.

'I... I don't know. I haven't really thought about it,' answered Roger, quickly looking around to make sure no one had heard the girl's rather indiscreet question.

Sylvia brought her face closer to his and a powerful but not unpleasant scent of perfume invaded his senses. 'I think you will, and you deserve it. You may not think so, but you're really good at what you do. And he knows it too,' she added, nodding towards the back of the gentleman who'd just announced his retirement. She gently pinched Roger's arm.

Once again he found himself hypnotised by the brilliance of those big, green eyes.

There was no doubt about it; he was noticing the girl more and more as she went about her business. It was that wonderful mane of hair and those fascinating eyes which made him weak whenever they locked on to him. And she certainly made sure he looked into them more often as time went by. Whenever she passed his desk he was treated to a broad smile and a spellbinding stare which turned his legs to jelly. It was a very new and a very disconcerting experience. Roger began to feel like a hooked fish, fighting hard to struggle free, but gradually and irresistibly reeled in by a stronger and much more determined force.

And he didn't know what to do about it. Life so far hadn't included the fairer sex, and although Roger had naturally experienced stirrings of a sexual nature, he had yet to act upon them. His social life left little opportunity for meeting young women as it was, well, dull to put it mildly. More often than not it was a soft drink at the local chess club with his few friends. The place was a male enclave, and rarely did a girlfriend or wife cross its threshold. It was true to say that even if a female had been there and taken notice of Roger, it would almost certainly have escaped his attention, focused as he was on the sixty-four squares arranged before him. In the past work had presented no opportunity either as, before Sylvia, there were no females under the age of fifty, which was why he supposed she was so noticeable.

He certainly did notice her early one Monday morning when, after only just arriving at the office, she made a beeline straight for his desk before he had time to bury his nose in the resident piles of paperwork.

'Do you like opera?' she asked, smiling bewitchingly at him.

'I… I don't know. I've never been,' he stammered, trying to avoid gazing into those piercing eyes.

'I guessed you hadn't. It's fantastic. You'll enjoy it immensely.' With a flourish of her beautifully manicured hand she plonked a large, white card firmly on the desk in front of him. 'You can pick me up at eight o'clock sharp – don't be late, as the place gets crowded. I'll give you my address later.' With that she smiled once more, turned and, hips swaying, sauntered off.

His mouth agog, Roger stared down at the invitation occupying centre stage on his desk. After a while his eyes focused on the blue print.

Madam Butterfly, an Opera by Puccini. Performed by the Barchester Operatic Society at the Alexander Theatre, Barchester. Monday, 28 January 1970.

He looked up to see Sylvia smiling sweetly at him from the bank of filing cabinets.

People in the office couldn't quite believe it at first. Quiet, polite, unassuming Roger, thought to be a confirmed bachelor and recently promoted to an associate of the practice, was dating the striking clerical assistant. That had been a turn up for the books, the sly fox.

The reality was somewhat different. Sylvia was dating Roger. She took the nascent relationship by the scruff of the neck and organised the hapless bachelor's social and professional life for him. Strangely, he didn't mind. In truth, he rather enjoyed it. She'd breathed life into him, and dragged him out of his wishy-washy way of life. It was as if he'd been given a purpose, something to aim for. His appearances at the chess club became less frequent, his attendance at the opera and theatre increasingly regular.

Aunt Mavis was delighted one Friday evening when Sylvia asked her if she could 'bring her friend Roger round for tea'. Of course, replied her aunt, intrigued. The 'friend' made an immediate good impression on Aunt Mavis with his quiet ways and good manners. His profession and prospects also sat well with her, and she could see that her niece was delighted with her catch. She definitely approved. Sylvia had blossomed into a lovely and popular young woman since going to work for Fleesem, Robsem, and Crooks. Just touching twenty years of age, she'd regained all the self-confidence lost after the disappearance of her father and the collapse of her mother. (Sadly, her mother never got to see the budding relationship reach full flower. In 1970, at the age of fifty-four, confused and broken-spirited, she passed away in the peaceful confines of St Mary's Sanatorium, Milverton.)

Their courtship was to last for the next four years. In 1974, after much hinting and prompting from Sylvia, Roger finally plucked up the courage to ask her if she would marry him. Her answer was an emphatic, 'Yes, darling. Of course I will. I've been waiting for ages for you to ask me.'

So in March 1975, after a small wedding ceremony conducted at St Peter and Paul's Parish Church, Barchester, followed by five days' honeymoon in blustery Scarborough, they found themselves temporarily settled in Aunt Mavis's home. Borrowing Aunt Mavis's ancient Morris Oxford, they immediately set about searching for a property that was within their joint financial means, and very quickly found, fell in love with, and bought a delightful 1930s semi-detached house in the outlying village of Comberton.

There was only one more thing in their young life that would make it complete. They needed their own car.

When the assemblers pieced me together in Coventry there were so many of us British – all makes, shapes, sizes and colours. We went to homes throughout the length and breadth of the land, and the car industry was one of the few that the nation had left to be proud of, although even then it was in decline. The makers packed us up and sent us off to many parts of the world, although the Yanks thought we were too small and puny for their tastes, and couldn't understand why we were designed to go around bends at a respectable speed without toppling over. Back then you didn't see many French, Italian or German makes – and the Japanese were considered a novelty. My, how things have changed. There are now Swedish, Spanish, Korean and even Malaysian makes on our roads and astonishingly we British don't have our own makers any more!

My life started on a long, rolling conveyor, assaulted by the competing sounds of banging, whirring, whining, whistling and assemblers shouting and swearing at each other. This was during an era of almost full employment in the car industry, with many guaranteed a job for life. Generation followed generation and sometimes even worked on the same line – grandfathers, fathers and sons. Job security wasn't an issue – job satisfaction was. History records the great industrial disputes that took place between the assemblers and the managers.

When the assemblers took it upon themselves to aggravate the managers (which they did frequently and with great gusto) there was nothing for us cars to do but sit there, partly made and half naked, and wait. According to the manager's plan I should have been assembled and checked over in six days. Not surprisingly, owing to sporadic and chaotic stoppages, it took ten.

'Not another red 'un 'arry. Wot the 'ell's got into poiple nowadize?' bawled one overweight, sweaty assembler in a thick Birmingham patois as I stopped directly opposite his bulging beer gut.

'Just a fad oi reckon, Ted. It'll goo awhy,' screamed back his Black Country mate from the other side of the line, disinterestedly screwing wheels on to my waiting hubs. 'Me, oi loike the blue. Too many of these red buggers abowt.'

'Know what you mean 'arry. Loike these Sprints thow… not that oi could afford one on the measly dosh they pay us in this 'ell 'ole.' The beer gut spat on his grubby hands, farted, and took another swig from an oil-smeared bottle of Tizer balanced precariously on the lid of his battered toolbox.

'Yeah, though oi did 'ear there's another stroike on the cards for this week… something abowt a bloke in the paint shop being forced to wear some sort of mask to protect 'is lungs. Did you ever? Now where did oi put that effin' inch Whitworth?'

'Bloody cheek! What'll them buggers think of next? Poor bloke won't be able to breathe proper if 'e 'as to wear a mask. They need takin' down a peg or two, them managers! Reckon if they troi that one 'e'll need more inconvenience money. Then we should get more as 'e's on the same grade as us!'

All of a sudden, the shrillness of a piercing voice cleft through the harsh cacophony as a tall, thin figure came striding along the line barking instructions at the assemblers.

'Right lads! Down tools! Right now! Meeting in the canteen in five minutes. Be there or be square!'

Within seconds a stream of grumbling, perspiring assemblers fell into line following the shop steward, like so many rats captivated by the mesmerising tune of the Pied Piper. The line slowly ground to a halt.

British Leyland, the country's largest maker, was having big trouble. The assemblers had had it too good for too long. Tired of constantly arm-wrestling with them, the managers had grown weak and ineffective. The lines on which we were made were forever stuttering to a halt as assemblers were instructed to stop working at the slightest perceived provocation. Half the time even the assemblers themselves weren't sure of the reason for a stoppage. They just did what the shop stewards told them to do.

You may have heard of a story about the Triumph TR7, the sports car paraded as 'The Shape of Things to Come' which went like this:

'The Shape of Things to Come' (another one-liner coined by the marketing men) quickly became the shape that came and went, in a great cloud of 'good riddance'. The doorstop-shaped TR7, and its rare V8-powered sibling TR8, were the last Triumphs sold in America and among the last cars British Leyland made before it folded in 1984. The trouble was not simply the engineering, or the peculiar design which looked fit to split firewood. It was mostly that the cars were so carelessly put together by the assemblers. The TR7's electrics suffered innumerable short circuits. Carburettors had to be constantly tuned to stay in balance. Timing chains snapped. Oil and water pumps refused to pump and would only suck. The sunroof leaked and the concealed headlights refused to pop open. One owner reported that his car's rear axle 'fell out'. How did that happen? It was as if British Leyland's assemblers were single-handedly hell-bent on sabotaging the country's balance of trade.

So you can imagine what times were like: troubled and turbulent. Assemblers blamed managers for poor sales and managers blamed assemblers for poor quality. An over-simplification, but that was what it boiled down to. The result of this was constant friction and a complete breakdown in the relationship between the two parties. Everyone's morale nosedived. And the consequence of this was poor attention to detail by the designers, too much focus on cost by the accountants, and a slapdash approach to construction by the assemblers.

The inevitable outcome was that many of us cars were defective at birth. Sometimes worse. Some were stillborn on the production lines and were towed away to an unknown place never to be heard of again. Some had to undergo extensive surgery as teams of fixers and fettlers searched, poked, prodded, and scratched their heads thinking of reasons why something wouldn't fit, or wouldn't work, or was simply missing without explanation.

I was one of the lucky ones. This was due to the fortuitous fact that I am a 'Special Edition', and the largest maker took extra care with the 'Special Editions' in order not to tarnish his image with those drivers who were prepared to pay way over the odds for the privilege of owning one.

When finished we 'Special Editions' were taken by the big carrier directly to the main agent, and awaited collection by our driver. Not so the standard models. Their route to the driver was much more tortuous.

For example, the largest maker's managers would decide that in a particular week they 'somehow felt' there should be so many standard cars produced as follows: 30 per cent red (seems popular at the moment); 20 per cent blue (sold well last year); 20 per cent white (nice colour for summer); 15 per cent green (everybody else seems to be making them in that colour); 10 per cent black (older drivers always like black – a legacy from the days when no other colour was available); and 5 per cent grey (somebody always asks for it – God knows why). The managers termed this a 'build to stock' forecast. So the lines geared up to produce this mix.

At the same time the main agents would collect firm orders from drivers and send them (not all at the same time mind you) to the largest maker. The largest maker would aggregate all the orders to get an overall picture of what had to be supplied from stock. They would then know how well they had done in getting the mix right with their 'build to stock' forecast.

So what happened when the forecast was compared with actual demand? The result was often not quite as expected.

Demand for cars: red (Ferrari had released 308GTB for UK sale, and wasn't Rosso the colour to die for), 50 per cent; blue (everybody had it last year, so boring), 15 per cent; white (gets too dirty, too quickly), 5 per cent; green (do I look like a Morris Minor driver?), 10 per cent; black (who wants to look as if they're driving a hearse?), 5 per cent; grey (nice and bland, you can't go wrong), 15 per cent.

Oops.

Do the maths and you can see the problem. Not enough red and grey cars and an abundance of every other colour. So what happened to all those colours excess to expectation? They were sent to the fields.

The fields. In spring or summer being sent to the fields afforded the unwanted cars an opportunity to chill out and shoot the breeze as they relaxed in their serried ranks, far away from prying eyes. On sunny days they bathed in the warmth of the shimmering orb, dull, waxy bodies soaking up the heat. But it wasn't much fun in the autumn and winter. On rainy days, they shivered under the constant putter-putter of freezing rain as they huddled together, trying to get warm. There were a lot of rainy days.

They remained in the fields until disturbed by the random arrival of the big carrier. Then there would be a flurry of activity as the loaders paced the rows searching for particular colours to hump on to the back and into the underbelly of the big carrier.

'Says 'ere we need three green, two white and one black, Bert. Now where's the black 'un?' questioned a loader, scanning the fields from under a beanie hat which shielded the mid-morning sun from his eyes.

'Over there, Joe. Look, there's one between the two grey and the blue. Bloody miles away as usual. There must be some law which says the ones you need are always the furthest away,' complained his fellow loader.

And with that the loaders would commence their game of search-and-find like a fast-forward game of chess, up and down the rows hunting for the right colour. And true to those militant times, after not too much searching, the promise of a good skive in the warm sun far away from the observing eyes of the managers was irresistible.

'Bugger this for a game of soldiers, Bert. I'm too hot to go hunting for some bloody car when I should be taking it easy at my age. Red Robbo should be down here watching what we 'ave to do. It's not right. 'e'd 'ave us out tomorrow, 'e would.'

'Red Robbo' – the most militant of the shop stewards. The scourge of the managers. The bloke who was to become the most powerful and destructive worker in the whole of the country.

Derek 'Red Robbo' Robinson had chosen to exert his iron grip on the tender testicles of the largest maker. He was officially chief shop steward of British Leyland's sprawling Longbridge assembly plant in Birmingham. With his network of irritable shop stewards in forty-two different car plants around the country, he master-minded a long-running campaign of strikes around the largest maker's empire in protest at the apparent mismanagement which, he claimed, was driving the car maker into oblivion.

Between 1978 and 1979, Red Robbo was credited with causing 523 walkouts at Longbridge, costing an estimated £200 million in lost production. As weak as they were, the managers resolved to remove this particular thorn from their sides. He was eventually sacked by British Leyland in November 1979. The damage already caused was irreparable.

'That's sorted those wankers out, lads. Next time it won't just be down tools – it'll be a full-blown strike.' With those words the tall, gaunt man made a two-fingered salute in the direction of the executive offices, conveniently located in a plush new building directly facing the grim, grey largeness of the assembly plant.

A cheer went up from the dense crowd that was packed like sardines into the grubby works canteen off to one side of the now-silent line.

'Good on yer, Tom. They'll think twice next time!' yelled a supportive voice from deep within the grimy ranks.

'Thank you, brothers, for your understanding. However, I am not convinced that those pig-ignorant tossers have enough nous to learn their lessons. So be vigilant and watch for any signs of skulduggery they may indulge in.' He raised a bony, clenched fist high into the air. 'Yes brothers, we shall overcome!'

A thunderous roar arose as the massed assemblers caught the mood of the shop steward. As it reached a climax he signalled for the crowd to be silent. Smoothing back a thatch of unkempt, steely-grey hair with knobbly, stick-like fingers, he cleared his throat, proceeded to fold his arms in front of him and looked earnestly at the multitude.

'And now, brothers, we are in for a special treat. We have an important visitor today who is going to tell us about his plans for the future of this plant.' He unfolded an arm and animatedly gestured towards the doors of the canteen.

'Your brother, Derek Robinson!'

All eyes swivelled towards the place where Red Robbo stood, his arm raised in a Hitleresque salute to the workers.

'Robbo! Robbo!' roared one of the assemblers, and the mantra was soon taken up by the mass until it filled the canteen and exploded into the assembly hall to echo round and round the vast empty spaces.

'Robbo! Robbo! Robbo!'

I didn't really want to be red; my preference would have been blue. Anyway, it didn't matter what I would've wanted as none of us cars had any say in the matter. That was determined by a far higher authority: the driver.

'It has to be red,' Sylvia stressed to the attentive man sitting behind the chrome-and-glass desk opposite her, in a tone that brooked no argument. Red was Sylvia's favourite colour and she wasn't often to be seen in any other. Red shoes, red dress, red coat, red hat – any shade from pink to crimson.

Blue was the one colour that found no favour with Sylvia.

'An excellent choice, Mrs Bunting, I would have made the same myself.' The sharp-suited salesman wisely decided to take the toadying route. He'd dealt with people like Sylvia before and had learnt from experience that if there was one kind of customer you didn't try to put one over, it was the Sylvias of this world.

'Blue's nice,' chipped in Roger, quietly. 'It goes well with cream upholstery. Looks fantastic. Absolutely gorgeous. You'd love it Sylv, I know you would.'

'But blue's such a cold colour, darling, and cream would mark very easily. I think the red would be much better.'

'You're entirely correct, Mrs Bunting,' agreed the salesman. 'Cream marks very easily as people often find to their cost.'

'Exactly, Mr Catchemall. It wouldn't be the best choice.'

The salesman had also met many Rogers in the course of his daily work. He knew they needed to put up some resistance to their spouse in the presence of another male, if only to demonstrate who really wore the trousers in the marital relationship. The salesman was much too canny to be fooled by this show of bravado. He knew who wore the trousers. And the shirt. And the shoes. And the rest of the wardrobe.

'Cream's easy to clean with the right stuff,' persisted Roger.

'I'm sorry, darling, I disagree. And I know you wouldn't like a dirty seat. Now that lovely grey fabric would be much easier to keep clean.'

'Ah, just what I was going to suggest, Mrs Bunting. The standard upholstery material can get dirty easily and ruin the entire appearance of the car. For just a few pounds more it's worth going for the brushed nylon,' prompted the salesman with a you're-not-going-to-win-here-mate look at Roger and a keep-going-missus-it-all-adds-to-the-price-and-therefore-my-commission thought in his mind.

'Fluff stands out on the grey, Sylv. I'll be forever vacuuming,' pleaded Roger, with a sideways please-don't-do-this-to-me look at the salesman.

'But you love vacuuming, darling. It's your favourite chore. You're particularly good at it. You keep the house really spotless. Don't forgo the pleasure of doing the car as well.' Sylvia smiled sweetly at Roger and made a to and fro movement of her hand as if gripping an imaginary cleaner and sweeping it up and down a dusty carpet.

Roger glared at the salesman who was desperately trying not to snigger.

And so it had continued. Ping pong, pong ping, ping pong until the colour/fabric rally was over. There could only be one winner.

Roger strived to save face. He may have been outgunned on the main decisions, but he was not prepared to roll over without scoring at least one point.

'We'll need a roof rack. And chrome mirrors,' chipped in Roger, without thinking.

Sylvia was magnanimous in victory and knew she would be much better placed for getting her way in future if she didn't make Roger lose face. So she gave him a little leeway now she'd had her way on the significant decisions.

'Of course, darling. What marvellous suggestions. Now if you gentlemen don't mind I'll leave you to sort out the paperwork. I feel a pressing need to go to the loo. Where is it please, Mr Catchemall?'

That's how I came to be red with grey fabric upholstery.

'Nice motor. Who on earth would put a roof rack and those stupid mirrors on it?' puzzled a technician at the main agent's. 'Like giving a Beatle a crew cut!'

'Probably some frumpy old couple who shouldn't have bought the car in the first place. No doubt conned by Catchemall. That man could sell ice cream to the Eskimos. They should've bought an Allegro instead... in green!' joked another technician. 'Still, no one will mess with this 'un. I watched the blokes in Coventry flogging one round the test track. Bloody wonderful sight.'

Oh dear. Now with Roger's additional 'bits' I would certainly look different. My colour, sporty lines and muscular power would go unnoticed; it would be the oddities – roof rack, those chrome mirrors, and (to be added later) a canary yellow AA badge – which would become an excuse for a good old laugh among the less well-mannered of the drivers.

But I was young and youth couldn't care less. I had dreams of streaking along the roads cutting a dashing figure as I zoomed past the less-blessed, with the wind howling over my aerodynamic wings and my powerful engine revving hard as I effortlessly overtook everything in sight.

I could barely contain my excitement when I thought of meeting a BMW 2002 for the first time.

Perhaps I should explain.

My great, great grandfather, Triumph Herald, was a distinguished and highly praised automobile. Conceived in the late 1950s, Herald was styled by that great Italian designer Michelotti. Michelotti produced beautiful designs for a pretty two-door saloon car with an innovative construction. Herald's main body tub was bolted to a chassis, and the whole front end hinged forward to allow full exposure of the engine. This made it very popular with drivers capable of doing their own servicing, as everything was so accessible, ease of repair being a strong plus. Every panel – including the sills and roof – could be unbolted from the main car. Styling was modern with a bright interior, thanks to a large glass area. Herald was considered easy to drive with light steering and controls, and excellent visibility, becoming highly popular as a driving-school car. Drivers also enjoyed preferential insurance premiums because of the Herald's proven inherent safety. Herald became a legend in its own time.

Herald's offspring was as much a failure as Herald was a success. In fact, it was so bland that Triumph didn't even bother to give it a name, deciding instead to label it simply Triumph 1300. 1300 did not have the aquiline features of its parent, being rather squat with a pug-nosed front end. Successive generations of blandness were to follow – 1300, 1500, Toledo – until Triumph once more came to its senses in 1972.

In that year, Triumph Dolomite was launched. In calling the car Dolomite, Triumph reused the name of a pre-war range of cars that were known for their sporting nature and technological advancement. Dolomite was aimed at the new compact performance/luxury sector, and was offered with a high level of standard equipment, including twin headlamps, a clock, full instrumentation, luxury seats and carpets, a heated rear window and a cigar lighter. The new Dolomite was good, very good, but still not as good as that mighty Teuton – the BMW 2002. Triumph then made a bold move. For once it took the shackles off its designers and put them on its accountants. The outcome was pure brilliance – the Dolomite Sprint, unveiled in the summer of 1973.

This is how the marketing men introduced me to the world:

'The Dolomite Sprint's compact overall dimensions belie a really roomy interior and also endow it with excellent manoeuvrability for town driving and ease of parking.

'The wide front seat and sofa-size rear seat, with fold-down centre armrest, are trimmed in luxurious brushed nylon, a hard-wearing, stain-repellent material that's warm in winter and cool in summer. The front seats are adjustable fore and aft and for rake with reclinable squabs and headrests. The driver's seat is also adjustable for height, and with a steering column that is adjustable both vertically and axially, there is a tailor-made driving position for everyone. The vinyl door trims match the seats and the floor is covered in deep pile carpet, while the rich walnut veneer of the comprehensively equipped fascia is also used for the door cappings. Inertia reel seat belts are fitted to both front seats.

'The heating and ventilation system is regulated by controls situated in the centre of the fascia panel, below which there is an adjustable air vent. In addition there are variable direction fresh air vents at each end of the fascia.

'At the heart of this Dolomite is an 1854 cc overhead camshaft engine which gives the car brisk, sporting performance with remarkable economy. A four-speed synchromesh gearbox is used, with overdrive as an optional extra. To complement the Dolomite's excellent road holding it has servo-assisted brakes, fade-resisting disks at the front, and self-adjusting drums at the rear.'

In plain English I was a wolf in sheep's clothing.

BMW was stunned. The mighty 2002 was in danger of losing its crown.

New Home (1975)

Before I was made Britain had many individual makers – AC, Alvis, Aston Martin, Austin, Austin Healey, Bentley, Bond, Bristol, Daimler, Elva, Fairthorpe, Ford, Hillman, Humber, Jaguar, Jensen, Lagonda, Lotus, MG, Morgan, Morris, Reliant, Riley, Rolls-Royce, Rover, Singer, Sunbeam, Tornado, Triumph, Turner, TVR, Vanden Plas, Vauxhall, and Wolseley.

Not surprisingly, there were too many makers chasing too few drivers and worst of all they made cars the drivers didn't want to buy and tried to sell to them at too high a price. Something had to give.

In 1952 two leading makers, Austin and Morris, came together to form the British Motor Corporation, BMC. In 1966, BMC merged with Jaguar to form British Motor Holdings.

Meanwhile Leyland Motors, which made commercial vehicles, acquired Standard and Triumph in 1961, forming Leyland Motor Corporation the following year. Rover, which specialised in luxury cars, merged with Leyland Motor Corporation in 1967.

In 1968, after a series of upheavals, Leyland Motor Corporation merged with British Motor Holdings to form British Leyland Motor Corporation, which became the largest maker in the United Kingdom. Ignoring lessons learnt in the past, BLMC continued making cars that nobody wanted to buy – with the notable exceptions of the Morris Minor, and the Mini, a brainchild of the genius Alec Issigonis.

By the late 1960s Japanese cars were being sold in the UK. They were cheaper than us. Funny that, as they had to be shipped at a high cost all the way over here. But what made the drivers buy Japanese cars as opposed to us? Simple. They went on sale at a highly competitive price and what's more important they came as standard with a radio, flashing indicators, a decent heater, and groundbreaking technology like a rear screen heater.

At that time most of us didn't have rear screen heaters. The drivers had to go to an accessory shop and buy a stick-on thing. Radios were expensive and an extra and so on. So the drivers looked at what was on offer with a Japanese car (usually at much less cost) and bought them. (Although arguably at first they did look a little more quirky in their appearance than we did, and this probably worked in our favour.)

There was a new kid on the block.

On 11 August 1975 the Government took over British Leyland, bailing it out of a financial crisis.

I narrowly escaped a premature termination.

On a chilly, cloudless day in late September I waited nervously with the others, arranged in a semicircle on the tarmacadam forecourt of BLMC's main agent in Barchester. I had arrived two days ago and was immediately dewaxed, cleaned, polished, fitted with those incongruous mirrors and roof rack and treated to a thorough inspection by the main agent's pre-delivery crew. I felt good, really good, and was in a mood to make conversation with the others around me.

'Mine's picking me up today,' I said with pride as I addressed the white Rover 2200 TC parked next to me.

'Mm.'

'Can't wait to go for my first real run.'

'Mm.'

'Stretch the legs, you know – give it a real go. Show them all what I'm made of.' I quickly looked around and whispered, 'Especially those BMWs.'

'Mm.'

'Yes, I'm really up for it.'

'Met him have you, your new driver?' The white one spoke at last. I detected something corrosive in his tone that made me a little hesitant in replying.

'No, not yet. He's picking me up today. I'm terribly excited about it.'

'Mm.' There was a return to the monosyllabic. He clearly wasn't the chatty type, but I didn't want to be silent, not on such a momentous and thrilling day as this. My first driver! The words filled me with pleasure every time I said them to myself. My first driver!

'When are yours arriving?' I was determined to get a conversation going with the Rover, despite his reticence. As soon as I'd asked the question I regretted it. My friendly enquiry was hurled back at me.

'Are you blind? In case you haven't noticed, I'm not exactly brand new.' He flexed his bodywork slightly as if encouraging me to take a closer look.

'Oh, I'm sorry. You look so shiny, you could have fooled me.'

Wincing visibly, his attitude changed to one of self-pity. 'It's amazing what two kids with a sponge and chamois leather can do to you. I'm aching all over thanks to Bob-a-Job Week. It should be banned in my opinion. It's a danger to life and limb.' He shrugged a little as if to illustrate the insensitive treatment he'd received at the hands of a couple of overzealous ten-year-old boy scouts.

Looking at him directly I could see sadness in his headlights. 'Did something happen to you?'

'Did something happen to me? Do you really want to know? I'll tell you what happened to me. I was an unwanted birthday present. Yes, hard to believe isn't it? Unwanted! Me, the top of the range! It didn't work out quite as I expected. My driver put in an order to the salesman as a secret surprise for his wife on her birthday. He was so thrilled when specifying all the extras – the salesman must have really thought his boat had come in! What my driver didn't know was that his beloved was well into an extramarital affair and had already decided to leave him. She confessed to the relationship one week after they collected me from here.'

'But don't drivers do things like that? I'm told they can be a little… unpredictable,' I ventured in my naivety. 'Not like us cars, of course. We've got much more sense. Thank heavens for the Code of Conduct.' (I'll tell you more about the Code later.)

'Sadly, they are very unpredictable. In ways you would never, ever imagine, I can tell you! In a wild rage after one blazing row he took a hammer to me and put me in the body shop for six weeks. Six weeks! I can still feel the dents and splits even now, and the pain I suffered when they tried to put me right. Excruciating!'

There was little I could say. It would be no consolation to remind him of the cars that succumbed to the dreaded mechanical sickness every day; of those that were stillborn on the production lines (oh yes, very few cared to remember that); of those that had to be painfully cured as the fixers and fettlers got to grips with their manufacturing problems; of those that died, horribly and tormented on the road; and saddest of all those consigned to the scrapyard either through terminal injury or plain old age.

'Look out, these two may be yours,' he whispered. 'Like the hat – reckon you've got a real pork pie there!' Oddly, he seemed to have perked up all of a sudden. I followed the direction in which he was looking across the tarmac expanse of the forecourt. My spirits sank.

Please, don't let these two be mine! They couldn't be, surely? Oh, no.

In my dreams I imagined a trendy, young couple; my driver sporting a slick moustache, luxuriant sideburns, tight pale blue jeans and a knee-length sheepskin coat. His girl coiffured with a French roll, wearing a figure-hugging sweater, and the shortest of miniskirts. A trendy couple who would be ogled wherever they went. Those were the type of people suited to me.

Instead, I got my very first sighting of the Buntings. Him: pinstripe suit, mirror polished black brogues. Her: floral print, court shoes, petite red leather handbag. My oil ran cold.

'I say, Sylv, what an absolute stunner,' whooped the suit, sidling up to me and running his gloved hand over my passenger side wing.

'Yes, darling. A lovely colour, and the upholstery matches perfectly, doesn't it? Just like I said it would. Much, much better than having chosen blue and cream.' Floral print patted me gently on the bonnet.

'Absolutely, Mrs Bunting. I said so at the time if you remember?' piped the salesman, who was trailing Sylvia at a respectful distance. Then, in a conspiratorial aside to Roger, 'Zero to sixty in nine seconds, Mr Bunting, and a top speed of nearly

120 miles per hour. It's also got an exhaust note to die for.'

'Great,' crowed Roger. 'I can't wait to take it for a spin and see what it's capable of!' He was grinning like a naughty schoolboy and almost jumping up and down in anticipation of the driving thrill to come.

Perhaps this is going to be fun after all. Fantastic!

My excitement didn't last very long.

'Oh no, darling, you mustn't drive it too fast. It's got to last us a long time,' reprimanded Sylvia, 'and we wouldn't want to give our new neighbours a bad impression by racing around. Come along, let's take her home. Have you the keys please, Mr Catchemall?'

'They're in the office, Mrs Bunting. All we have to do is get you to sign off the delivery paperwork and it's all yours,' explained the smug salesman.

'In that case we'll follow you. Come along, darling.'

With that, floral print, the suit and the salesman about to put down a healthy deposit for his holiday in Barbados (courtesy of the Buntings) turned around and headed off in the direction of the showroom.

'We wouldn't want to give the new neighbours a bad impression, would we?' mimicked a green MGB parked next to me.

'Zero to sixty in nine seconds, but we'll take twenty instead as we wouldn't want to be seen to be tearing around,' teased a big, black Jaguar XJ12 next to the MG.

I shrunk my bonnet into my wheel arches under the joking. Why me? What had I done to deserve these two? The likes of the Buntings didn't buy cars like me. They bought slow, plodding, sensible models like the Marina, not sporty models that strained to be given their head on the open road.

'See you back here in a month, then?' sniped the Rover, with an impish sparkle in his headlights.

I never saw any of them again. By the time I returned to the main agent for my first service they had all gone to God-knows-where.

Against all expectations I was to remain with Roger and Sylvia for a long time. A very, very, long time.

My new home was one of a number of solidly built semi-detached properties dotted in regulation around a quiet crescent in Comberton, a medium-sized village some twelve miles from Barchester. The village nestles against the side of a gently undulating series of hills which meander down towards the sea three miles or so distant, where they transform into a small valley, wooded and without any river. In these parts this kind of valley is known as a 'coombe', and many of the place names contain the word 'coombe', as do many of the house names.

Coombe View was situated in the approximate middle of the crescent and had uninterrupted views across open fields of grass to the rear. On one side of the house, flanked by a dense privet hedge, ran a long gravel drive, which hugged the boundary and wound its way gently down past a well-manicured lawn to a pebble-dash garage. The drive was protected from the road by a pair of wrought iron gates.

As was her wont, Sylvia had taken the initiative and declared she would be the one who opened and closed the gates. 'Mind the gatepost, darling. Left a little. Slow down. Stop. STOP!' she shrieked, standing stock still and pointing a slender forefinger like a gundog's tail magnetically stuck on the location of a lead-riddled pheasant. 'You nearly touched the gnome! You were *that* close.' To stress the point she indicated just how close by holding the first finger and thumb of her non-pointing hand millimetres apart.

Ah, the gnome. One smug little bugger. In those days they seemed to be everywhere you looked. Everyone's garden demanded at least one gnome to be fashionable. Some truly eccentric folk collected dozens. Gnomes were caught in frozen poses – more often than not fishing, wheeling barrows or cutting wood. People pictured them as an industrious race of tiny folk, never stopping in their toils, like tireless ants scuttling around purposefully on a sun-baked patio. This accounted for their popularity, as they radiated the Victorian work ethic held in such high esteem by the better-off in seventies society. (All was not as it appeared, I later learnt. It was alleged the gnomes really had a terribly poor attitude to work, and it was rumoured they gathered in gossipy, indolent gangs when all the lights in the houses had been extinguished for the evening.)

Sylvia had succumbed to the gnome disease within one month of moving into Coombe View.

'Yeah, watch where you're going, kid. I'm the boss around here,' hissed the gnome under his copious beard as I stopped within inches of him. 'The sooner you accept that the better. You may be *his*, but I'm *hers*, and you'll soon get to know what that means, see?' He glared threateningly at me for a twinkling of an eye and then resumed his lifeless staring.

'I'm miles away, Sylv. Stop worrying. I'll be careful.' Just to be on the safe side Roger reversed a little and had a second attempt.

Being a callow youth I was tempted, sorely tempted. My steering is a little slack, not manufactured to the same close tolerances as the modern generation, and I would have had the perfect excuse. Roger, not being the brightest of planners, had also positioned the gnome in a rather vulnerable position, right on the edge of the drive adjacent to the gatepost. The gnome's eyes widened as I judged it to perfection, sliding past his overly large, pockmarked nose and missing it by a whisker.

'Sorry Sylv, I'll soon get the hang of it. Don't worry,' comforted Roger while inwardly heaving a sigh of relief. No doubt the gnome was doing the same.

The gnome and I never got on after that. I was a happy-go-lucky youngster, always in a bit of an adventurous mood. That was precisely what the designer intended when he penned the first sketches of me.

In stark contrast the gnome was sourness personified, destined to squat in the same position day after day with that ludicrous fishing rod in his hands and vacant look on his ruddy, bearded face. Spring, summer, autumn, winter. No umbrella, no sunshade, no smile, no fishing to while away the time. (His fishing line had already disappeared by the time I came to live at Coombe View, and Roger's pathetic attempt at building a mortar pond for the gnome's fishing was full of cracks – it had never held water even when first built – so fishing was out of the question, even if the line were to be replaced.)

It didn't bother the gnome. He didn't give a tinker's about fishing. Or wheeling barrows or cutting wood for that matter. None of them did. What would they do with wood anyway? It wasn't as if they had any houses to build, or fires to light. No, what the gnome really enthused over was getting together with his cronies in the oily darkness of late evening and getting pissed on the potent, muddy grog that only gnomes know how to brew. It was after a few mugs of the thick, cloudy liquid that their real nature bubbled up to the surface.

'Fishing, we'll show 'em effing fishing! Wheelbarrows, we'll tell 'em where to shove their frigging wheelbarrows! Cutting wood – what's the point in that? We'll show 'em what fucking gnomes can really do!' they choroused when they all got together in their little clique among the rockery plants at the darkest end of Number 32's garden. It was quite uncanny how they returned to their predetermined positions the next day, even before the milkman arrived to do his rounds. But if you looked closely enough, and it was a miracle no human ever did, you could see evidence of their excesses in bloodshot eyes with dark rings around them. Some were even bold (or drunk) enough to carry out mischievous deeds as soon as the milkman had departed – a favourite being the smashing of vulnerable milk bottles left on front doorsteps. The neighbourhood cats always got the blame for this.

I'm not entirely sure myself of all the things they really did get up to, as I was always carefully tucked away in the garage. But their giggling and crude obscenities often filtered through the walls as the night wore on. Oddly, I was the only one in the household to notice how over the years the gnome's nose grew fatter, redder and even more pitted, and his already outsize paunch continued to travel south. I imagine the garage knew what went on as all the garages looked out for each other and had unknown ways and means of communicating gossip, rumour, and hearsay.

I almost felt sorry for the gnome. Almost, but not quite.

The garage always had a tale to tell me of course, and he loved to go on at great lengths. In those early days I never quite learnt to separate fantasy from reality as far as the garage was concerned.

'Heard about the Spitfire at Number 44? Lost her temper last week in Wales and intentionally – intentionally mind you – had a puncture. Half way to Welshpool in the middle of nowhere! And on Sunday, to boot! And that's not the worst of it. She let the air out of her own spare tyre as well. Can you believe it?' The garage was in his element when he had a juicy tale to tell.

Letting the air out of the spare tyre was a favourite trick of ours when we were in a bad mood, or had been stressed or upset by our driver. It was easy, very easy, and very effective. One minute going steadily along the road, the driver whistling away happily. The next... pssst!... psssst!... pssssssssssst! A hissing of air followed by a low rumbling and stomach-churning flappety-flap as the tyre speedily deflated. We had learnt through experience gained over generations NEVER to do this when in the vicinity of a garage; NEVER when in the middle of a town; NEVER when aid from passing motorists was available; and NEVER EVER when in sight of an RAC or AA man.

And the fun we had when we heard the driver trying to explain away the state of affairs!

'I can't understand it. We've been on a smooth road for miles.'

'I can't find a damned thing wrong with the tyre. Why it's gone flat I don't know.'

'That's bizarre. The spare's flat too.'

And, oh, the way we rolled from side to side during the arguments that invariably ensued.

'Why didn't you check the tyres before we came away, dear?'

'Didn't you check the spare, dear? I'll bet you didn't. Typical of you!'

'What are you going to do now then, dear? Tell me, what are you going to do?'

Oh yes, a very mischievous trick and, as I said, very effective.

'The Ford Escort told me it was the driver's fault she threw a fit,' I said to the garage, coming back to my senses. 'He hadn't checked her water for weeks, she hadn't been washed for ages, and he hadn't replaced a broken indicator bulb. Escort said it was making her miserable, and she wasn't starting first time in the mornings.'

Simple explanations were insufficient for the garage. The tale begged to be beefed up, laid out, and served with more than a dash of spice.

'What does the Escort know? He'd believe anything she told

him! She can wrap him round her little tie rod! That's not how it was. No, no, not at all. She's a little imp that one. I heard from a reliable source that the driver wanted to go touring in Wales, but she wanted to take them shopping. She loves shopping, you know, could spend all day going from one shop to the next.' The garage would brook no other explanation, so I nodded, accepting his interpretation of the story rather than starting an argument.

In truth my interest was always aroused by the Triumph Spitfire. She certainly was a sexy little thing. Curves in all the right places. Beautifully sleek and shiny – and when she went topless, well, all the other male cars in the area started to run hotter and hotter.

'She certainly worked it well,' continued the garage, determined to milk the story for all it was worth. 'Ended up with her driver having a blazing row with his wife. They didn't speak a word to each other for three days after they returned. What a minx that Spitfire is!'

That set me to thinking of the coming holiday in Scarborough.

'Have you double checked you've got everything, darling?'

'Good gracious, for the third time, Sylv, yes, I have.'

This was to be their first holiday after the honeymoon. A tradition was about to be born. A tradition which grasped uncertainty, impatience and anxiety with both hands and mashed them all together.

'Did you pull the plugs out, darling?'

'Yes.'

'Locked the back door?'

'Yes.'

'Packed the sunglasses?'

Pause for thought. 'Er, no.'

'Oh, Roger, how many times do I have to tell you?'

Roger fumbles for door keys. Unlocks front door. Opens front door. Wipes shoes on mat. Takes shoes off. Puts slippers on. Ascends stairs. Opens drawer, closes drawer. Opens another drawer, closes drawer. Opens wardrobe, closes wardrobe. Opens bedroom window. Puts head out.

'Where did you say the sunglasses are, Sylv?' The question floats over to her from the protruding head above.

Irritated tut-tutting from my passenger seat. The question is ignored.

'Sylv. Sylv. SYLV! WHERE DID YOU SAY THE SUNGLASSES ARE?'

My door opens quickly. Heels click Gestapo-like on the drive. She doesn't answer Roger's shouting.

'SYLV!' Then he spots her, hands on hips glowering up at him. He's stopped in his tracks. He knows that stare.

Closes the bedroom window. Descends stairs. Takes slippers off. Puts shoes on. Enters from the front door. Looks pleadingly at her.

'Have you done telling the whole neighbourhood we're going away on holiday?' she chides, hands still on hips.

'Sorry, but I can't find the sunglasses.'

'Did you try looking in your side table middle drawer? The obvious place?'

Inwardly curses. Why hadn't he thought of that? Of course it was the obvious place, of course it was. Bugger!

Sighs deeply. Turns around. Re-enters house. Takes shoes off. Puts slippers on. Ascends stairs. Opens middle drawer. Retrieves sunglasses. Closes middle drawer. Descends stairs. Takes slippers off. Puts shoes on. Closes front door. Locks front door. Hurries over to me. Opens my door. Slithers in. Puts seatbelt on.

She's waiting, arms folded.

'Did you pack the suntan oil, Roger?'

'Bugger!'

And the whole ritual would be repeated, often several times. In fact, my own patience was frequently tested as I sat waiting for the torture to end. This time it took almost ten minutes with all the toing and froing. In later years it could go on much longer.

I'll never understand why I felt so puckish on that particular day. Looking back I can only blame it on a need to experiment, to test the boundaries. The prank I had in mind was simple, but very effective. A piece of pure mischief. The driver always got the blame with this trick, so I would never come under suspicion.

'OK, Sylv. Last check. Money? Map? Hankies? Socks? Undies? Shorts? Shirts? Shaver? Anything else?'

'No, Roger, that's all your things. Mine are all packed. All my cases are fine. Everything's checked on my list. Now can we go, please?'

'We're off, we're off, and we're off in a motor car.' (Roger always bursts into this banal ditty whenever in a holiday mood.)

Turns the ignition key.

Whirr… whirrrr… whirrrr… whirrrr.

Stony silence. I'm bursting, trying to keep the smirk off my grille.

Whirrrrrr… rrrrr… rrr… rr… rrr… rr… rr… r… r… r… r… r… r.

Click. Click. Click. Click. Click. Click.

'I think the battery's flat, Sylv.'

Click. Click. Click. Click.

'Definitely no oomph in the battery.'

Click. Click.

'I'll leave it for a couple of minutes.'

Thirty seconds later.

Click.

'I'll try again.'

Nothing. Not a sound. Not even a click. Dead.

'Er, I don't think it's going to start, Sylv.'

You should have seen my self-satisfied look. I don't know why I hadn't tried it before. Of course, 'Special Editions' weren't supposed to be unreliable, but threatened with bankruptcy the largest maker had been more careless than usual of late, offering the perfect excuse for our breaking down. It wasn't our fault if on occasion we used their ineptitude as an excuse.

'What are you going to do, Roger? We're expected at the hotel at five.'

'Let me think, Sylv. Er, well. Er, actually, I'm not sure.'

'What are the options, Roger?'

'Options? Hmm, options. I, um, er… I suppose, er, um, er…'

'Option one?'

'Cancel the holiday? Er, no I can see you don't like that. Er…' An uncomfortable pause ensued. 'What do you suggest, Sylv?'

'Option one, Roger. Call the AA?'

'Ah, yes, yes. Excellent idea. I'd forgotten all about the AA. Yes, of course.'

'Option two?'

'Option two? Let me see. Ah, yes. Call the hotel and tell them we'll be a little late this evening?'

'Exactly. Now go and carry out options one and two. I'm not going to sit here all day, I might as well make a cup of tea. And the next time we go on holiday you might care to check the battery first.'

They open my doors in unison. Get out. Sylvia clicks across the drive. Roger puts key in front door. Unlocks front door. Opens front door. They both wipe shoes on mat. They both take shoes off. Roger puts slippers on. Sylvia slips mules on. Pink mules depart for kitchen. Blue slippers depart for lounge and the phone.

'Hello? Is that the AA? Roger Bunting speaking. My membership number? Er, hold on a minute, please.' Fumbles in wallet. 'Yes, it's here. 371632. Problem? Er, yes. It's the car. Won't start. Where am I? I'm at home. Sorry? What do you mean I'm not covered if I break down at home? A different class of membership? I thought there was only one? There's an extra charge? How much?' Sweat breaks out on Roger's forehead as he calculates the cost of his inattention to the small print on the AA contract.

'And you can't upgrade my membership until next week? But I need assistance now! Pardon? There's an emergency charge for that, given my circumstances? I see. How much is that then?' Rivulets are now running down Roger's temples.

'Is there a problem, Roger?' asks an invisible voice from the kitchen.

'No, no, Sylv. It's OK. It's all in hand.'

'Do you wish to proceed, sir?' queries a tinny voice from the phone.

'Do I have a choice?'

'Not if you want your car seen to today, sir.'

'Will your man take a cheque?'

'Sorry, sir, no cheques. Cash only.'

'OK. Then I'll go ahead.' Roger's heart skips several beats as the financial commitment is made.

'Address please, sir. Yes, I have that. Someone will be with you within the next two to three hours. Thank you. Have a good day. Goodbye.'

The next two to three hours. It was ten o'clock now, and the journey to Scarborough would take some six hours. Assuming that the AA man came at one o'clock and took an hour to sort out the car, they could be at the hotel just on the strike of eight o'clock. Cutting it fine.

'Have you rung the hotel yet, Roger?' The invisible voice once more.

'Just about to, just about to.'

'Hello, is that the Castle Hotel? It's Mr Bunting here. I'm afraid we'll be delayed slightly this evening. Problem with the car. Is that all right? Oh, good. What's that? Will we be requiring dinner? I think so, yes. What time do we expect to arrive? About eight o'clock I hope.'

'Sorry, sir. The last seating for dinner is at seven thirty.'

'Oh, dear. I see. Yes, yes, no problem. If we're late then we'll have to make other arrangements. Goodbye to you, too.'

'I do hope this gets sorted soon, darling. I'm so looking forward to a romantic dinner this evening,' says Sylvia as she enters the lounge and snuggles up next to him on the sofa.

The clock on the mantelpiece shows ten minutes past three o'clock. They are on the fourth cup of tea of the day. The sun has decided to hide in the clouds and there is a light drizzle puttering against the glistening window panes.

Ding, dong. The doorbell rings.

'Would you get that please, Roger? I can feel a nasty headache coming on.'

'On my way, Sylv.'

'Hello, sir. I'm from the AA. I believe you have a problem with your vehicle? Sorry I'm late, but it's been a beggar of a day. You wouldn't believe how many call-outs I've had today. Unbelievable.'

'Oh dear, I see. I'll come out. Would you like a cup of tea?'

'Kill for one, sir. Two sugars, thanks.'

Roger turns and heads for the kitchen. The pink mules are beating out a steady tap-tap-tap on the linoleum. This habit, Roger has realised, is something that has been encoded into his new wife's genetic make-up. During their courting he learnt to be constantly alert for the warning signals transmitted by this subconscious activity, like a manic woodpecker persisting in cracking open a concrete lamp post. Pity was he'd not yet discovered how to approach her in a way that could guarantee there wouldn't be any repercussions.

'The AA man's arrived.'

'So I see. Did you ask him how long it will take to fix?'

'Er, I didn't.'

'Why not, Roger?'

Silence. Blue slippers slide cautiously over to where the kettle is. 'I'll just put the kettle on. Back in five minutes. Do you want another cup of tea?'

Silence. It could have been the middle of the Mojave Desert.

Blue slippers beat a hasty retreat to the front door.

'And don't forget to take your slippers off if you're going outside.' That invisible voice again, following his withdrawal from the kitchen.

Takes slippers off. Puts shoes on. Walks across the drive.

'The car appears to be locked, sir. Do you have the keys?'

Audible sigh from Roger. Returns to the house. Takes shoes off. Puts slippers on. Pads across carpet to understairs cupboard. Removes keys. Pads back across carpet to front door. Takes slippers off. Puts shoes on. Walks down the drive again.

'Here they are. The larger one is the door, the other is the ignition.'

'Thank you, sir. Let's give it a whizz, shall we?'

'It won't do any good. I tried for ages this morning. Flat as a pancake. In my opinion, the alternator's gone belly up. Might as well tow it to the garage now. Even if you jump start it we'll only be in the same position tomorrow.'

'Yes, sir, I understand. Would you please stand back so I can get in?'

I wish they'd seen my grin. The first time I made use of the power I had to control my driver. I'd kept Roger waiting in nervous anticipation, stomach knotted, counting down the minutes as he awaited the long-overdue arrival of the AA man. Now the time had arrived. My moment of triumph. The killing of the bull. It was time for the coup de grâce.

The AA man turns the ignition key.

Vroooom!

First-time start.

Roger stands there jaw-droppingly speechless. The AA man looks at him in an another-bloody-idiot-wasting-my-time way.

'Well, that's very strange,' bleats Roger, a look of startled incredulity spreading over his face. 'It wouldn't start this morning. It really wouldn't. I tried for ages. It just wouldn't start. It just wouldn't.'

'Doesn't appear to be the alternator, does it, sir? We'll switch off and try it again.'

Turns off the engine.

'OK, here we go.'

Vroooom!

First-time start again.

'Do you mind if I try it?' asks Roger, still in disbelief.

'It's your car, sir. You go right ahead.' The AA man turns off the engine and climbs out of the car allowing Roger to slide in behind the wheel.

Turns the ignition key.

Vroooom!

'I would say it's perfectly OK, sir. Must have been one of those gremlins. Now if you don't mind I've got a couple of stranded drivers to attend to. Can we sort the cash out? Oh, and any chance of that cup of tea?'

There is an atmosphere thick with tension as they settle into me for the second time that day. The AA man has departed, having had three cups of tea, bored them rigid with tales of vehicles he's brought back from the dead, trodden oil into Sylvia's new Persian rug, and relieved Roger of £50 (leaving him short of cash for the holiday, so an unplanned visit to the cashpoint will be required).

'So why didn't you try to start the car again before the AA man arrived? We're late, we won't be having our dinner this evening, and I've a ruined rug. Don't you ever THINK?' At this point Sylvia bursts into tears, and she begins to shake uncontrollably. This is something I've never previously witnessed, and it distresses Roger visibly.

This was not the outcome I had intended. Sure, playing the prankster was a novelty for me, and the thrill of mischief was something I'd relished – before things went as far as they had. It wasn't as if Roger and Sylvia are inconsiderate or negligent people. Every Saturday morning, then as now, regular as clockwork, I'm lovingly washed, dried, inspected. My oil and water levels are checked, tyres pressures checked, with pumping up if needs be, and then the bit I most like – the vacuum cleaner smoothes my carpets and upholstery. My, how erotic that is!

Roger always ensures that I go to the main agent for my periodic service, and I believe this is undoubtedly the main reason for my longevity. If there is ever the slightest concern with regard to a piece of my anatomy, it's immediately repaired or replaced. Yes, you don't know how painful it is to have your brake pads worn, or suffer a dud spark plug or, worst of all, have your ignition coil causing misfiring. It makes my washers leak thinking about that!

I'd been stupid, and not thought through the consequences of my actions.

So I felt guilty, really guilty.

But you wouldn't want us cars to be predictable now though, would you?

Contemporaries (1975)

You may know some of my contemporaries – Austin Maxi, Morris Marina, Triumph Stag, Austin Allegro, Leyland Princess, Triumph TR7, and Jaguar XJS – although you'll be lucky to spot many of them on the roads today. Oh, but don't think they've all been consigned to the scrap yard. Far from it.

An ever-decreasing number of us oldies are still used as day-to-day transport. But the vast majority are destined never again to see the light of day. All over the country you'll find us squirreled away, many by the collectors of this world. Lost and forgotten in some old barn or garage, gathering dust and cobwebs and gradually rotting away in the way of all things neglected. And then there will only be memories, and apocryphal reminiscences from the collectors. Thank heavens for the collectors. Quirky they may be, but without them we oldies would be nothing but dull cubes of scrap metal waiting to be reprocessed. God bless the collectors.

In those days in the 1970s – unlike today – drivers had particular loyalties to certain makers and they would rarely consider changing. You could almost match the maker with a driver if you knew the driver's circumstances. For example:

Austin Maxi – the car for the conservative driver, likely to be in late thirties/early forties. First choice of teachers and vicars.

Triumph Dolomite – for those who wanted a sporty image but had to contend with the needs of a young family.

Morris Marina – the sales rep's car. Who would ever buy one out of their own pocket?

Triumph Stag – one to die for. The Stag was, and still is, breathtakingly beautiful. Unfortunately she had a fatal design flaw (poor attention to detail by the designers again) and her unreliability quickly earned her a bad reputation. Disgruntled Stag owners loyal to the brand often turned to the Triumph TR7 – a much blander and even worse-designed car.

Austin Allegro – the eccentric driver bought these. You'd have to be, with a rectangular steering wheel!

Leyland Princess – the executive driver's choice. Probably middle management in their early- to mid-fifties with a grown-up family.

Triumph TR7 – drivers who desired a Triumph Stag but couldn't afford one. Young, upwardly mobile, predominantly male. Junior lawyers, executives, and professionals of all kinds.

Jaguar XJS – the choice of the well-to-do with nothing-better-to-do. Playboys, landed gentry, and rock stars.

Amazingly, there weren't that many female drivers back in those days.

The poor quality of cars being designed and built by the makers led to a rapid growth in those assisting the drivers in times of difficulty – the AA man and the RAC man. There should never have been any need whatsoever for these gentlemen. Had the designers done their job properly, the accountants been less focused on cost, and had the assemblers carried out their tasks with due care and diligence, the makers would have produced dependable cars with a healthy lifespan.

The world, however, is not perfect. The world of the British motor car was far from perfect. Our cars were, to put it kindly, flawed. The drivers grudgingly accepted this. They'd never known anything different – until the Japanese arrived on these shores. Those clever, industrious and extremely well-organised Orientals had waited a long time for their opportunity. After suffering the humiliation of defeat in the Second World War following an astonishing start to their campaign at Pearl Harbor, the Japanese had rethought their assault on the world. This time they made the wise decision that if they couldn't succeed by force, they might by excellence in manufacturing, showing the big industrial nations how to design, make and build products that were of very high quality and competitively priced. They'd demonstrated their technological ability during the conflict, and many times were in advance of the Americans, the most powerful industrial nation on earth. They had the foresight to analyse things patiently, carefully and critically; take things apart, see what could be done better, and develop innovative and sometimes groundbreaking manufacturing processes.

In 1958 Honda introduced its first model in the United States, the Honda C100 Super Cub motorcycle (called the Honda 50 in the UK), which still holds the title of being the best-selling vehicle in history, with around 50 million units sold around the world. The Super Cub was geared to providing cheap urban transportation in busy cities. It triggered the eventual domination of the world motorcycle market by the Japanese, and contributed greatly to the rise of their car industry.

The Japanese car makers bided their time. They were in no hurry, and were fortunate in having such sons as Kiichiro Toyoda, founder of the Toyota Motor Company which was destined to become the benchmark for quality to which all other car makers aspired. Their assault on the UK began carefully with the introduction of the Honda S600 to the UK in 1967. Its specification was more akin to a Formula 1 racing car, with a tiny 791 cc engine revving to almost 10,000 rpm giving it a top speed of nearly 100 miles per hour. Incredible.

Other models were soon to be imported into Britain from Datsun, Toyota and Honda during the next decade. The cars had excellent build quality and reliability, being let down only by their bland and unappealing styling, with a few notable exceptions such as the Datsun 240Z, which was to completely change Datsun's image.

The Japanese had shown what they were capable of and the world sat up and took notice. They learnt their lessons on styling and applied them. Offering cars that didn't break down and were crammed full of 'extras' that came as standard, they were hampered only by restrictive quotas that countries such as the US and the UK imposed upon them. As creative as ever, the Japanese even found a way around that.

I remember my first encounter with one of the Japanese.

It was on a stretch of the recently upgraded Barchester bypass, known locally as 'Hammerton Straight' on account of its three miles of undeviating, perfectly horizontal road. Hammerton Straight was too inviting to be resisted by any driver who happened to stumble across it. Even the most docile were sometimes tempted to see just how fast their cars were capable of going. Back in the seventies, for all but the most exotic of cars, the magic figure to reach was 100 miles per hour. 'The Ton.' If your car could do The Ton on Hammerton Straight it was something you could brag about to your pals. Provided, of course, your pals weren't in the pay of Her Majesty's Constabulary.

Roger was not immune to the seduction of Hammerton Straight. Though it was not a route he normally took when accompanied by Sylvia, he found himself one fine sunny morning with the opportunity to take the bypass on the way to returning me to the main agent for my second service.

At the beginning of the straight there was a large roundabout that collected the traffic from the small towns and villages that lay to the south of Barchester. Having negotiated the circulatory, Roger entered the tempting stretch of road, and a tiny clutch of genes inherited from his Uncle Alf kicked in. As he gently depressed my accelerator pedal there was a whoosh as a tiny red rocket rushed past me, yelling 'Banzai!'

What was that? I thought as I focused on the screaming banshee pulling away from me. Half my size, it was a car the like of which I'd never seen. I felt a sudden surge as my throttle was flipped opened. Roger had reacted. Gradually I began to catch up with the pocket rocket. 'Banzai!' it screamed back at me. 'Banzai! Banzai! You no catch me!'

It was a challenge no thoroughbred could resist. You little beggar, I'll show you, I thought. I concentrated hard as the oil began to flow faster and faster, and the revs built higher and higher. I was catching up with him! 'Banzai!' came the scream once more, and I couldn't believe the whine he was putting out. His engine must have been up at 7,000 rpm! The needle on my speedometer was going in one direction only – upward, seventy-five, eighty, eighty-five miles per hour. I could feel the grip tighten on my steering wheel and felt the heat increase on my driver's seat.

Then, unbelievably, he began to pull away from me again. 'Banzai! Banzai! You no catch me!' he yelled again, the whine now reaching an unbearable pitch. He must be doing almost 9,000 rpm. Why hadn't his engine blown up? What was I dealing with here? Ninety, ninety-five, ninety-eight miles per hour. I was fast gaining on him again, but I could see the terminal roundabout at the end of the straight looming in the near distance. Would there be enough time to overtake him? Could I do it? Would Roger have the courage?

Then – 100 miles per hour – we had done it. The Ton. But there was no way we were going to get past the little fellow. Roger hit my brakes. Ninety… 80… 70… 50… 30… 10. We pulled up behind the midget at the exit roundabout. Now I could clearly see the distorted 'H'. So, he was a Honda. I scanned his boot for further identification and on the bottom left-hand side above the circular rear light cluster I saw it: S600. Then off he zoomed again in the direction of Milverton while we turned off on the road leading to Barchester.

Honda was destined to become the largest and finest maker of engines the world had ever known. The Japanese had arrived.

Early Years (1975–80)

1975 was a landmark year.
  Margaret Thatcher became leader of the Conservative Party.
  The Yorkshire Ripper killed his first victim.
  David Beckham was born.
  Charlie Chaplin was knighted.
  Roger and Sylvia tried for their first baby.
  Sylvia had just passed her twenty-fourth birthday and was in her fifth year of employment with Fleesem's. The practice had been good to both her and her husband. Sylvia's efficiencies had been well recognised by all and she was now the senior clerk in Charities. Galvanised by his popular wife's success, Roger had found something unexpected and previously alien to him – ambition. Shortly after old man Fleesem's retirement, and exactly as predicted by Sylvia, Roger was offered an associate position in the Companies Division which he quickly accepted. The promotion did him the world of good. Shaken out of years of lethargy he now began to take an interest in what was going on around him in the workplace. He struck up friendships with colleagues who had previously merited hardly a nod from him, and took to making a point of saying 'Hello' to everyone he passed on arriving at work in the morning.

  Their social life picked up dramatically. They became friendly with people outside work through contacts among Roger's clients and as a result of Sylvia's membership of the local women's group. There was a whirlwind of dinner parties, theatre outings, weekend walks away in the West Country and visits to stately homes. The friends revelled in carefree, child-free, pet-free times doing exactly what young professional people do. Pleasing themselves.

  Then it happened. In August 1975 an invisible contagion started spreading among the Buntings' new circle of friends. Amanda Blake was the first to be struck down. It came as somewhat of a surprise when Amanda, stick thin and a proclaimed career solicitor, declared over dinner one evening that she and her engineer husband, Garry, were 'going to sprog'. There was a stunned silence as the startling news was taken in by the assembled company. Amanda had always and most vehemently proclaimed that 'We won't be having any children. Messy and troublesome things that they are.' And now here she was telling everyone she was pregnant, with a radiant beam on her mother-to-be face!

Strike one.

Not six weeks later as they were chatting at the bar in Barchester's Alexander Theatre, another of their circle, Ted Mortimer, a successful local Estate Agent, turned to the group and, putting a finger to his lips, shushed for silence. When he had their full attention he cleared his throat and said, 'Jayne and I have some very important news. We're going to have a baby.'

Strike Two.

The latest revelation was during the Ladies' Evening at Ted's Masonic Lodge. Well fed and slightly the worse for wine, Patricia Connery, a dentist practising in Grevington, giggled and blurted out, 'I know this sounds boring, but… what the hell… I'm pregnant!'

Strike three.

Within a few months, topics of conversation turned away from careers, cars, and clothes to babies, buggies, and bottle feeding.

Then Sylvia received a phone call from her younger sister, Lucy. Sylvia had been very close to her two sisters, Lucy and Jane, ever since her mother had died in a sanatorium after the Urquhart family lost their home. With help from Aunt Mavis she'd taken on the role of surrogate mother to the thirteen- and sixteen-year-olds. She helped them through the difficult teenage years; listened closely and sympathetically to their problems; and made sure they mixed with the right kind of boys. On many an occasion Aunt Mavis declared that Sylvia got away with things that Sylvia's mother wouldn't have done – not without a blazing row that is.

Lucy, a bright girl like her big sister, went away to Edinburgh University to study marketing. In her final year she met Charles, a vicar ten years her senior, whom she married shortly after graduating. Twelve months ago she'd secured a position as a trainee buyer with a reputable, national retail chain. Fortunately for Lucy (and Charles) her employer agreed for her to be based in Edinburgh.

Guess what? Lucy and Charles were expecting a baby.

Not surprisingly, Sylvia's thoughts turned to children. I say Sylvia's thoughts as Roger's were often elsewhere, his recent elevation to the status of associate at Fleesem, Robsem and Crooks being the most visited place. His dealings with influential business clients had awoken a realisation in Roger that bobbing along like flotsam on life's ebb and flow for the next thirty-odd years would not unlock his true potential. It finally dawned that he could, and should, be doing much better in his career. An added impetus came from the conversations he regularly had with Sylvia that had a habit of meandering their way back to the subject of babies.

Her hormones were crying out for something to lavish her affections on.

'Darling, I think we should seriously consider starting a family. We're not getting any younger, you know.'

It had been building for some time. Roger knew that Sylvia couldn't avoid being affected by the group of budding roly-poly mums-to-be. There was a constant dialogue of clinics, birthing methods, and decorating baby's room. Even the fathers-to-be had caught the bug.

'You're only twenty-four. There's plenty of time yet, Sylv.'

'Yes, but they say that women are in their prime for bearing children at eighteen years of age. My mother was thirty-five when she had me, and she said that was far too late. She said if it they hadn't been so busy with the business she would've had me much earlier. If we have children now, by the time they're grown up I'll still be relatively young.'

'Aren't you being just a little influenced by all our pregnant friends?' he questioned. 'It's bound to have an effect on you. It's only natural.'

'Don't you want children?'

'Of course I do,' lied Roger, knowing full well that he didn't really, but would never dare say so.

'Then we really need to start. And soon.'

For months after that Sylvia's sexual appetite went into over-drive: First thing in the morning, again after breakfast, as soon as they arrived home after work, and any time Sylvia was in the mood during the evening and when they went to bed. And she was always in the mood. At first it was great to have his fiery, wild-eyed wife riding him, gripped tightly between her long legs, but it quickly got to the point when it was wearing Roger out. Never a great one for physical exercise, Roger sweated, heaved, and puffed himself through the endless bouts of coupling. Mind you, it was doing him good. In three months he lost six pounds in weight, and had to lie to his colleagues at work that he was 'on a stringent diet'.

Nothing happened. Sylvia upped the work rate. Roger couldn't understand where she got her energy from. Maybe it was all those years of riding horses in her teens.

It continued for another three months. Still nothing happened. Roger lost another four pounds. It was killing him, and Sylvia was beginning to look very drawn. Clearly, sexual intercourse multiple times a day was not the answer.

'Sylv, this can't go on. There must be some sort of problem with one or the other – or both of us. Perhaps we're trying too hard.'

Sylvia burst into tears.

'It's me, I know it is. Everyone else is having babies, except me. None of our friends have had the slightest problem. It's not fair!' Clenching her fists she ran out of the dining room, up the stairs to their bedroom, and slammed the door shut.

Roger was shocked. He'd had to bear the brunt of Sylvia's temper before, but this wasn't a temper tantrum. This was something he'd experienced only once before. And then it had been my fault.

Maybe Aunt Mavis could help.

You may not know it, but we cars feel attracted to the opposite sex as well. Not in the same way as drivers, more like an aesthetic appreciation. (Of course we depend on the makers for reproduction. We can't do that ourselves. But that doesn't mean we don't have fantasies.)

I've already mentioned the Spitfire at Number 44. I couldn't keep my eyes off the Spitfire. None of us could. In her day there were very few that could match her curves, and as the garage was fond of saying, she knew it. Every time she passed we would slyly swivel our lights and watch her pass each one of us, knowing full well what effect she was having. In those days though, we all honoured the Code. Rule 6: Do not, ever, make any kind of improper advances to a car of the opposite sex. It could lead to a contravention of Rule 1: Never, ever reveal what sex you are to any driver. Break Rule 1, and no car would ever speak to you again. Ever.

Sly looks were all the Spitfire ever received, mind you. Back then all cars knew how to behave. We treated each other with respect, especially females and the older ones. If you saw a female or an old one waiting to enter the main road from a side road, we would always – without exception – flash our lights and let them in. It was second nature and we didn't think twice about it. It had been ingrained for generations. We always kept our distance, too. No matter how much the temptation to get close to the rear of a female car in front, we always maintained a sense of propriety and kept a polite distance from which we could admire the curves in front of us. The blasphemy 'rear end shunt' horrified us and cars would rarely voice those words.

It was the same for the female cars. Very few would tease us by going topless or waggling their rear ends on particularly winding roads. (The drivers wrongly assumed a swinging tail end was a problem with the car and they called this 'oversteer'. Absolute nonsense! There wasn't a car on the road that had oversteer. It was something the saucy female cars did to tease the males, and the males did to frighten the drivers.)

It's all changed now. Respect for the females and old ones has completely vanished. I can't remember the last time a car let me out of a side road, and the behaviour of the young males and females is unbelievable. They bunch up on the roads nose-to-tail in such a blatant way! 'Rear end shunt' has become accepted in our language to an unbelievable degree. Recently I even heard of cars breaching Rule 6. And guess what? Nobody gives a damn.

Aunt Mavis's heart went out to her niece. For almost three years now the Buntings had been trying for a baby, but without success.

Something was broken and nothing came of their repeated attempts to conceive. (This was in the days before IVF was freely available. Louise Brown, the world's first baby to be conceived 'in vitro', was born on 25 July 1978.)

In the absence of a viable alternative, Aunt Mavis advised there was only one avenue left open to them – adoption. However, Sylvia was strongly against adoption, on the grounds that 'You can never tell what the child will grow up to be like. If you don't know the character of the biological parents, how in heaven's name do you know what the child will grow up to be? It's too much of a lottery between a genius and a psychopath.'

Aunt Mavis conceded she had a point.

'Darling, did I ever tell you about the pony I had when I was twelve?' Sylvia asked Roger one evening when they were clearing away the dishes after their meal.

'You might have done. I do know you were interested in horses.' Roger tied the strings of his blue-and-white striped pinny, slid on a pair of bright yellow Marigolds and began to run washing-up water from the hot tap. He had an inkling of where this was going but chose to hear his wife out.

'Oh yes, I was mad keen at the time. Daddy' – and here she choked a little on the word – 'Daddy bought me a lovely pony that I named Henry. A palomino.'

'Is that a sort of blotchy horse, like the Red Indians have on cowboy films?' teased Roger, plunging the dinner plates into the frothing white suds.

'Not really, darling. Palomino is a coat colour in horse breeds. They have a gold coat and white or flaxen mane and tail. It's very attractive. In my opinion, it's the most attractive colouring for a horse.'

Thank God we don't have red horses, Roger was thinking to himself.

Sidling over to the sink she put her arms around his expanding waistline, and gave it a gentle squeeze. 'Darling, I was thinking,' she whispered in his ear. 'I did enjoy riding a horse. It's a skill you never lose. A bit like driving a car, I'd imagine. I'd rather like—'

'It would be a lot of hard work, Sylvia,' cut in Roger. 'You know that. Plus the fact that it would cost a lot of money.'

'Which we can afford, darling.' She inserted the tip of her tongue into the cup of his ear which sent a tingling sensation shooting down the side of his neck and into his groin. He flinched involuntarily and pierced the index finger of one Marigold with a fork.

'Beggar! Now it's leaking!' he exclaimed, holding the rubber glove close to his face and searching for the offending hole.

'Don't change the subject, there's another pair under the sink. What do you think, should we get a horse?'

It looked as if a horse was going to be their baby substitute.

Without doubt Henry Mark II was a striking equine specimen, seventeen hands high with beautiful Palomino markings. Sylvia had fallen in love with him at first sight.

Roger hadn't put up much resistance to the buying of the horse. If it meant Sylvia didn't think about babies then that was fine with him. It was destined, however, to bring about a change in their relationship of a totally unforeseen nature. The demands of the horse meant the Buntings rose early, grabbed a quick breakfast, then drove me to the stables where Sylvia fed and watered Henry, while Roger read *The Times*. They then joined the commuter rush and arrived at the office shortly before nine o'clock.

It couldn't last. It soon became apparent that the early morning routine was beginning to tell on both of them. Not the best of risers, Roger found himself yawning involuntarily during the first hours of the working day, a sight not missed by his colleagues. It was found to be most embarrassing when, attending a policy meeting with one of the partners and two of the associates, he nodded off during a droning monologue on one particularly dull agenda item.

'Am I boring you, Roger?' asked the partner, tapping Roger on the forehead with a pencil.

'Wha... what... er, no,' replied the dozer, shaking himself out of his semi-catatonic state. 'Sorry, Mr Crooks. I had a very late night last night. Sorry.'

Resolved not to let it happen again lest it be counted as a black mark against him in his aspiration to make a full partner one day, he decided he would have to have a frank discussion with Sylvia. He could think of only one way to solve the problem. She would have to learn to drive and they would buy a second car. The only other option didn't even bear thinking about. There was no way he could ask her to sell the horse.

The conundrum was that Sylvia had never learnt to drive. Not only had she never learnt but she'd never expressed the slightest desire to drive. Maybe that was because she'd always had someone to chauffeur her around wherever she went. First there was her father, then Aunt Mavis, and now Roger. Well, she'd just have to learn. An additional car would be expensive and sacrifices would have to be made, but the situation couldn't be allowed to carry on. He resolved to raise the thorny subject that very evening.

As usual, his wife was one step ahead. 'Darling, I've been thinking. I realise it's not on for you to take me to the stables every morning in a half-awake state. I can tell it's affecting your work. And I know you're not really interested in Henry, you just do it for my sake. So, I've been doing some thinking and I've got a proposition for you.'

Here it comes. She's going to suggest we get a second car. Well, that's fine with me, Mrs Bunting. I'm already on the ball with that one.

'I've been talking to Mr Fleesem and he said he'd be only too pleased to help,' she continued.

Fleesem? What in heaven's name has this got to do with the boss? Maybe he knows someone who's selling a car?

'He's quite happy if I work afternoons only, as long as Mrs Dewhirst and Mrs Carney are prepared to take on more responsibility. I don't think they'd have a problem with that as they're both extremely conscientious workers. Well, what do you think?'

For a moment Roger was incapable of thinking. This was a completely unexpected answer to the problem. Then the cogs of his mind slowly engaged and started to turn. His initial reaction was, no, no way. How would they manage on a reduced income? How would they be in a position to maintain the improving standard of living that they were now beginning to enjoy?

'You're very quiet?' she queried, with a frown on her face.

'I'm thinking it through.'

It wasn't such a bad suggestion after all, he decided. It would mean that there was no need to buy a second car and all the expense that entailed would be avoided. He could get back to his normal morning routine. Best of all it would enable Sylvia to nurture an interest outside of work. But there was one problem.

'I think it's a good idea, if you're happy with it. But if you go and sort Henry out every morning, how will you get there, and then how will you get to work?'

Sylvia smiled broadly. 'I've thought about that. You can drop me off in the mornings, later than you do now, of course. There's a bus from Lower Moreton to Comberton at nine twenty-five that I could catch. That would get me home about nine fifty. I can then change clothes and catch the eleven ten to Barchester. I'll be in the office before noon.'

Amazing, thought Roger. Why did I bother asking the question?

'That's a lot of buses. Do you really want to do that every day?'

'Oh, darling, it's really not much of an inconvenience. It means I can see Henry every day and not put you out of your way. What do you think? I think I should.'

On this occasion, Roger agreed.

Gradually, a schism was appearing in the Bunting's social circle. One clique polarised around the antics, incidents, and frustrations with their growing offspring; the other on careers, business, and shared interests. They all remained friends, but now instead of their social gatherings being all-inclusive they would split and gravitate toward different rooms or different tables to discuss their different interests. By the last year of the decade the split had widened considerably. Although the friends on both sides stayed in contact, their social coming together became less and less frequent.

The childless Buntings were introduced to a new crowd that had money and influence. New acquaintances invited them to parties at some of the grandest houses in the county, owned by some of the richest people. New money, old money, it didn't matter. Roger and Sylvia got to mingle with them.

On one of their social outings they were invited to the home of Conrad Quinney, the owner of a chain of furniture stores. Conrad was a divorcee in his late forties, tall with a military bearing, well spoken and very well connected. His family had been an important customer of Reginald Urquhart and he was well aware of the circumstances surrounding his disappearance. However, he had no idea that Sylvia was Reginald's daughter.

'Hello, Roger, glad you could come. This must be your lovely wife you keep telling me so much about?' Conrad opened the door to the Buntings and they ushered themselves into the spacious hallway of his large Georgian house.

'Hello, Conrad. Yes, this is my wife, Sylvia. Sylvia, Conrad. Conrad Quinney.'

'Pleased to meet you, Conrad,' said Sylvia, offering her hand to their host.

'Have you come far?' asked Conrad, flashing his broad smile at the young couple.

'Comberton,' answered Roger.

'A lovely village. I used to walk a lot on the hills around there with my daughters at one time. They're grown up now of course, so sadly I concern myself more with my business nowadays.'

'Were your daughters at Roedean by any chance?' queried Sylvia.

'Why, yes they were. Why do you ask?'

'I was at Roedean with two sisters named Quinney, but I didn't have much to do with them as they were several years younger than me. I remembered as it's such an unusual name.'

'Yes it is. Has its roots in Antrim, or so I'm told. Amanda and Caris both went to Roedean. One's a dentist in Manchester now and the other's just got engaged to a media executive. They're completely different characters but then, of course, children often are. I know quite a few parents as I spent several years on the PTA. I might even have known your father.'

Sylvia shuffled uncomfortably.

'What was his name?' continued Conrad.

'Urquhart. Reginald Urquhart.'

You could have heard a pin drop. Sylvia and her host stood silently looking at each other and appeared to be considering the revelation they'd just made. Roger coughed nervously and shuffled his feet, expecting an unpleasant reaction. On other occasions when people connected Sylvia to Reginald there had always been an unpleasant reaction.

It was Conrad who spoke first. 'I did meet your father once or twice. He was one of my father's key suppliers. They did a lot of business together at one time. A very charming man, if I remember correctly.' Turning towards the lounge he beckoned them to follow him. 'Come along now, I'd like you to meet my other guests. There are some very interesting people here tonight.'

And so it proved to be. Conrad Quinney's circle of friends and acquaintances had an unbelievably large radius. Through him, the Buntings work and social lives underwent another metamorphosis. Conrad introduced Roger to his extensive business network. Through these contacts, Roger brought new and influential clients into the firm of Fleesem, Robsem and Crooks, to the amazement of the partners, who never thought that Roger would have it in him to actually 'sell' the firm to any prospective client. Of course, Roger didn't need to do any selling. Conrad did it all for him. In no time at all the Buntings were allowed into his inner circle, and visits to Conrad's home became a regular fixture on their social calendar.

As you might expect, I got to meet some very interesting characters as a result of the Bunting's burgeoning friendship with Conrad Quinney. There was Conrad's company car which he used only on business, a 1972 Bentley T, hand-made in the Rolls-Royce-owned factory in Crewe.

The Bentley wore his ancestry like a coat of arms and was rather up himself. 'Do you know,' he was fond of saying, 'I have royalty in the very fibre of my being. One can trace my lineage back to the earliest days of the motor car, unlike most.' The last two words were stressed, as if heritage by itself endowed him with a superior intellect and purer gene pool than his peers. This didn't exactly endear the Bentley to others and he was often baited on account of his better-than-thou attitude to those around him.

His stablemate was very different: a 1963 Aston Martin DB4 GT nicknamed 'Bertie' that was Conrad's passion. Bertie was a classy vehicle, and a tad schizophrenic. Charm simply oozed out of him, but he could be a real devil if he had a mind to be. That was what Conrad found riveting about Bertie. Docile one minute when tootling around town, then wild and capricious on the open road when Conrad stamped the throttle to the floor. So unlike the Bentley, who was unexcitable whatever speed he was travelling at.

Bertie hadn't much time for the Bentley, whom he called 'Benters', often with an 'old boy' appended for good niggling measure. 'Looking a bit peaky today, Benters, old boy.' 'Stuck in the garage again, Benters, old boy?' 'We're off for a spin round the jolly old block. See you later, Benters, old boy.' The Bentley usually rose above it all. In his opinion Bertie was simply in a lower class, even if he was quite rare. Sometimes, however, the Bentley couldn't help but take the bait.

The first time I met them was at one of Conrad's dinner parties. We were the first to arrive and Roger had parked me next to Bertie. Twenty feet away from me, on the other side of Bertie, the Bentley was tucked away in one of the three conjoined garages with its vertically opening door slid back high above his roof, and the evening sunlight shining on his blemish-free, deep blue paintwork.

'Wotcha, I'm Bertie,' the Aston greeted me with a broad grin on his grille. 'You are?'

'Mine call me Dolly,' I answered, sheepishly.

The Aston concealed a snigger and there was a muffled 'Hrmmmph' from the Bentley.

'Dolly?' enquired Bertie, the sniggering morphing into curiosity.

'Short for Dolomite. On account of my being a Triumph Dolomite, you see. My driver's wife thought it suited me. He didn't correct her.'

'Ah, Rule 1.' Bertie nodded his head sagely.

Yes, I know it's a girl's name. It was Sylvia's mistake to wrong sex me by shortening 'Dolomite' to 'Dolly'. It was just one more thing I had to put up with. Not that I blamed Sylvia. It is one of the closest guarded secrets that we cars have. Rule 1: Never, ever reveal what sex you are to any driver. It's a good rule. God knows what treatment we'd receive if we were known to be male or female. (To this day the sex of not one single car has ever been revealed to any driver. If you don't believe me just approach a driver – any driver – and ask him, or her, the sex of his or her car. I guarantee they won't have a clue.)

'Another of the working classes, eh?' floated a far-back voice from the direction of the house. 'No respectable heritage, whatsoever. Those Triumphs are as common as muck.'

'Don't mind him,' Bertie nodded in the direction of the voice. 'That's Benters. Thinks he's a cut above the rest,' then, raising his voice slightly, 'I say, Benters old boy, why don't you be civil and introduce yourself to Dolly here?'

'Hrmmmph. Hello Dolly. They call me… hrmmmph… the Company Limousine. Do you know I have royalty in the very fibre of my being? One can trace my lineage back to the earliest days of the motor car, unlike most.'

A sigh escaped from Bertie and he rolled his headlights.

'Oh come, come, Benters old boy. We've heard it all before. Everyone knows you're just a Rolls in drag.'

It was a sharp reminder that at that time Bentleys were held up as poor cousins of the Rolls-Royce. There was an indisputable truth in this – in the seventies Bentleys were genuinely Rolls-Royce clones. They really were a Rolls-Royce in drag.

'And everyone knows you're a Flash Harry. All show and no substance,' came back the retort.

I didn't know where to look.

'Don't mind Benters, he's not a free spirit like me. Look at his day. He's taken out of his garage by the chauffeur first thing in the morning and transports Mr Quinney to work. Then he stands alone in the company car park all day until he's needed. Then after Mr Quinney has been driven home from work, he's washed by the chauffeur and stuck away in his garage until the next day, when it's all repeated again. What a boring life.' The last sentence was thrown at the Bentley like a gloved challenge.

'Whereas my days are so varied.' He looked straight at me. 'Do you know what I've done this week, Dolly?'

'Do you want me to guess?'

'No, of course not. I'll tell you what my week's been like. Saturday, Mr Quinney – not the chauffeur, he's not allowed to drive me – drove me to Epsom races with his friend the Right Honourable Henry Montague, and Henry's sister and her friend. Mr Quinney didn't spare the horses! He had the ladies and the Right Honourable screaming with fright as we yawed and pitched around the rolling roads on the downs. It got my adrenaline rushing, I can tell you – as both Mr Quinney and I knew we were almost on the limit of our abilities. He's one to trust though, Mr Quinney. A fantastic driver.'

A pang of envy shot through me. If only Roger was a little more like this Quinney chap.

'Then on Sunday he took me for a spin around Silverstone with his friend Mr Moss. Mr Moss brought along Dino, a Ferrari. What a runner! I had real trouble on the bends with him, but on the straights he didn't stand a chance! One in the eye for the Eyeties!'

'Hrmmmph,' shot the Bentley. 'You're just a wastrel. Perhaps you'll grow up one day and accept some responsibility instead of fooling around.'

I could see Bertie enjoyed teasing the Bentley. What I later came to understand was that this was how their relationship worked. Every time I met them they went through the same routine. Bertie would play on his playboy lifestyle and the Bentley would berate him for his immature and irresponsible ways.

On another occasion Conrad had arranged to meet friends at Epsom races. This time the Italians were out in force. I had never been in the company of so many good-looking cars before. It made me feel quite plain.

They were certainly an exotic bunch, the Italians. Suave, handsome, and incredibly athletic. There were the Ferrari brothers – Dino, 308GTS and 365GTSBB; the Lamborghinis – or Lambos as they preferred to be known – Jarama, Urraco and Countach; and the Maseratis, Merak and Khamsin. Garrulous, sophisticated and utterly unpredictable. Bertie delighted in their company.

' 'Allo, Bertie. 'Ow issa eet witha you?' asked Dino, a grin on his grille.

'Fantastic, old man. And you?'

'Belissimo, belissimo. Ia luvva the 'orses. Who issa youra leetle friend?'

'This is Dolly.'

'Issa girl's name, no?'

'It's a nickname,' I quickly pointed out.

'Issa no matter. You enjoya yourself. Come anda meeta the boys.'

There is something about the rich isn't there? Confident, full of life, exuberant, carefree. Call it what you will, the rich are different. The Italians weren't just rich – they were super rich. So rich in fact that money was a dirty word. A common word. If you were awash with it there was no need to talk about it. So, they didn't.

I felt privileged.

A little way down the slope from Bertie and the Italians, and closer to the racecourse, a silver Rolls-Royce Camargue and a black Daimler Majestic were parked side by side. Both were looking down their long bonnets at the Italians.

'Flashy foreigners,' snorted the Rolls. It was said just a little too loudly not to be deliberate.

'Common as muck, no breeding,' added the Daimler, even louder.

The Italians and Bertie looked round to see where the snide remarks came from.

'I say, chaps, mind your manners,' remarked Bertie.

'Did someone squeak?' said the Rolls, pretending to hear a noise.

'Must be some rust on the old brake drums,' crowed the Daimler.

I gasped in disbelief. This was a flagrant breach of Rule 6: Always be polite and courteous to other cars. What I hadn't realised until then was there is one rule for the rich, and another for the rest of us. No, correction. The rich don't bother with any rules.

'I beg your pardon,' persisted Bertie. 'I think you'd better apologise to my friends.'

'Issa no matter, Bertie,' stated Merak, turning towards the pair. 'They issa just a pair of ignorant, olda farts.'

'What did you call us, you pile of tin?' shouted the Daimler.

'You hearda me, toffee nose. I said you anda your friend are a pair of ignorant, olda farts.'

'Come over here and say that, Eyetie. You won't be so brave then,' challenged the Rolls.

What happened next was testimony to the commonly held belief that those of a Latin origin are prone to having a quick temper. Merak must have released his handbrake and began, ever so slowly at first, to roll down the gentle slope towards where the tormentors were parked. It didn't take him long to pick up speed. Heading towards the Rolls I could see a wild look in his head-lights matched by a look of disbelief from the Rolls.

Looking back I can remember every detail of Merak's progress down the slope, almost as if frozen in time. Homing in on the Rolls, the bright yellow thoroughbred completed his terrible mission with an almighty bang, resulting in a direct hit on the rear of the Rolls. The momentum imparted was so great that the Rolls was shunted into an old, but classic, Bentley that was having sixty winks. The old gentleman was so startled that he too rolled forward and ended up nuzzling against the rear bumper of a dowager Daimler, who screamed with shock at the terrible violation of the hallowed Rule 2: Never, ever, make any kind of improper advances to a car of the female sex.

Pandemonium broke out with horns sounding everywhere. Drivers came streaming back to the slopes from the track, bewildered by what was going on. The Rolls was apologising profusely to the old Bentley that was berating him, while Merak was taking a chunk out of the Rolls boot.

Then there was a piercing sound as Dino's air horns sliced through the air. Before long all the Italians joined him. The noise was deafening.

(Did you know drivers think we have only a single tone when we blow our horns? Wrong. Their hearing isn't sufficiently acute to detect the full range of sounds we produce.)

The Italians were cheering.

Gone Missing (1980)

By 1980 the Saturday afternoon routine was well-established. Roger and Sylvia adhered to a schedule which was always the same, irrespective of the weather, time of year, minor local events, or major national catastrophes. At one o'clock sharp, they gathered their shopping bags and drove me into Grevington town centre for the weekly shopping trip.

I could drive to the county's second most important town on autopilot. Left off the drive, down to the end of Mornington Crescent stopping at the T-junction with Pedder Way. Right on to Pedder Way passing St Margaret's (an exclusive public school for young ladies) to the T-junction with the main road. (It pays to be very careful here. This is where the St Margaret's inmates play dares with the traffic.) Turn left on to the main road and keep going straight as a die for six miles until we reach the brown and cream Victorian bridge over the river which defines Grevington's town boundary. Take the first right once over the bridge into Tennant Street. Down Tennant Street past the Ex-Servicemen's Club, to the junction with Waterford Road. Wait at least ten minutes (this is a very busy junction). Join Waterford Road which then inexplicably metamorphoses into High Street. And the queuing begins.

Crawl slowly down High Street, past one, two, three, four, five left turns. Then it's upon you. Tolpuddle Gate. The muscular street that shoves you into the giant multi-storey. Turn into Tolpuddle Gate and enter the gaping mouth of the concrete monstrosity which contains five floors – Ground, and Levels 1, 2, 3, and 4.

At this point I come off autopilot and try to guess the next move. What will Roger do? There are several interesting possibilities:

1. Head for the nearest vacant parking space on Ground Level, and park there.

2. Find the nearest vacant parking space on Ground Level, but be informed by Sylvia that the cars parked in the adjacent spaces are 'too close for comfort' and try elsewhere.

3. Drive immediately to Level 1, which is the level for the Marks & Spencer store entrance.

4. Drive right up to Level 4 (open air, top level) as all the other levels may be full anyway.

5. Drive to any level, except Level 4, as it's raining.

Come on, Roger, decision time. Please don't end up on Level 2. I don't like Level 2.

And here's the reason why. Ground is bright and open and bounded on two adjacent sides by a busy footpath that is a main thoroughfare from the riverside promenade to the town centre shops. No matter what the time of day you can be assured that pedestrians will be in abundance on this arterial route. Cars can see the pedestrians, and the pedestrians can see the cars. Ground is safe.

Level 1 affords easy access to the rear entrance of Marks & Spencer, and offers the magnetic draw of the cafeteria. What better place for drivers to have a cuppa before indulging in the joys of shopping? No matter what time of day (Sundays excepted) you can always be assured of drivers meandering through Level 1 en route to and from M&S. The drivers can see us and we can see the drivers. Level 1 is safe.

Level 3 contains the hut for the multi-storey watchman. It's his job to keep an eye on us. Unfortunately, and for some unfathomable reason, the owners of the multi-storey prefer to employ the old, arthritic, asthmatic, or just plain lazy. The result of this is that the watchman takes a very myopic view of his (never her) duties and responsibilities. His domain appears to be limited to Level 3, although on occasion it might extend to Level 1 if he needs to pop into the town centre via M&S for a bit of nosh (the M&S cafeteria is too expensive). This is never done via Level 2 – he takes the backstairs route thus bypassing Level 2 – and exits into the hustle and bustle of Level 1. Level 3 is safe.

Level 4 can be seen from a large neighbouring C&A, and it's a long haul on foot from Ground. On a really hot day Level 4 is akin to the Danakil Depression; in midwinter to Siberia. When it rains you run the risk of being drenched before you can make the shelter of the stairs. Waiting for the creaky and urine-stained lift is not an option. Level 4 is safe, if not exactly inviting.

Level 2. Oh, the poor, unloved, neglected Level 2, trapped between busy Level 1 and secure Level 3, it offers neither protection nor comfort. Local cars dread Level 2, and drivers have no idea about the fears brought on by Level 2. How could they?

On this particular Saturday afternoon it was raining, and Level 4 was closed for some remedial resurfacing work (of course, nobody was working on a Saturday afternoon), so Roger's options were limited. I hoped we would end up on Level 1. I hoped in vain. Level 1 was chock-a-block.

'There's one – over there. That'll do,' ordered Sylvia.

You guessed it. We were on Level 2.

'No problem, Sylv,' as Roger manoeuvred me into a space lacking adjacent neighbours.

'Don't forget to lock the car.'

'I won't. You know I always do, darling.'

Yes, he always does. Without fail. And he did so on this occasion. As they left me and walked to the stairs to disappear behind the fire door, I felt a growing apprehension. I hoped this was unfounded. After all, Level 2 is only a stone's throw from the hustle and bustle of Level 1. Why worry?

Three bays away from me a big Mercedes S500 was having the same thoughts.

'I do not like zis lefel,' he whispered to me. 'Zere iz mischief here, mark my verds.'

'You're imagining things,' I replied, coolly. 'We're as safe here as anywhere.'

'You know and I know zere is alvays a problem on zis lefel. Ze drifers don't know zis. But ve cars do.'

I tried not to dwell on his troubled words and instead took to mentally counting off the miles on my milometer, a habit I had developed in times of stress.

Absolute silence. You could have heard a pin drop.

As I reached one thousand three hundred and thirteen there was an almost inaudible creak from the same exit door that Roger and Sylvia had used. Several of the lights on this level had blown and not been replaced and, as little daylight filtered in from outside to brighten the insides of the building, there were patches of inky darkness sprinkled all around Level 2.

A patch somewhere developed a voice. 'Ere, Gaz, wot about the Merc? Fancy that then, eh? Dead tasty,' whispered a squeaky falsetto.

'Nah, we'd never fence that, mate. Too bloomin' obvious. Nice motor, though. Let's have a shufti for summat a bit less flash,' advised a cracked, husky bass.

'OK, Gaz. Like wot?'

'Rover, Triumph, Vauxhall. Common stuff. Nuffink foreign.'

'OK.'

My temperature gauge began to rise. Where were the voices coming from? What were they up to?

Then I caught sight of two shadowy figures flitting in and out of the unlit areas. They were sneaking around the few cars parked on Level 2. I heard an occasional dull clunk as they cautiously, ever so cautiously tugged car door handles to see if a careless driver had left their car unlocked.

After five minutes or so, during which not one driver came into or went out from Level 2, everything went quiet again.

I breathed a sigh of relief. Thank goodness they hadn't found any doors open.

'Wot about this one, Gaz? Nice motor, these.'

I froze as a clammy, hot hand fingered my door handle.

'Yeah, the man'll like this, Baz. Easy to get into. No alarm, see?'

No alarm. Not surprisingly, in 1975 the largest maker's accountants in their infinite wisdom decided alarms were too costly. Even on us 'Special Editions'. Not necessary, was the verdict. Car theft would never be a problem in this country. It wasn't like America, and never would be.

I felt a tingle as a cold, looped wire was slipped over the top of my closed driver side door window and slid expertly down to engage the knob of the door locking mechanism.

'Gently, gently now,' coaxed the rough voice.

'You're good at this aintcha, Gaz? A real artiste!'

'Shhh! Every bugger'll hear you!'

As the locking mechanism was raised, the clammy, hot hand yanked the door handle and click! My door was opened.

'Get in quick! I'll wire the motor,' the rough voice ordered.

Suddenly I felt a sharp tug on my ignition wiring like the sting of an angry wasp. Then I jumped as the wires were shorted, forcing my starter motor to turn and springing my engine into life. My body had been invaded!

'Gotcha! Have you found the ticket?'

'Yeah. It's here. I'll never know why the silly sods leave them in the car. Do you?'

'Nah. Makes the job easy, don't it?'

I gasped as I was viciously hurled forward out of the parking bay.

'Blimey, clutch is sharp on these!'

No, no. This couldn't be happening to me. I shot a glance at the Mercedes as we went around the perimeter of Level 2, but he avoided my look. Down the ramp to Level 1 we went, a little more carefully this time (I assume so we didn't get noticed by any other drivers), around the perimeter of Level 1 and down another ramp to Ground. Straight across the middle of Ground, then pulled up sharply at the pay booth.

'Ticket please, sir,' requested the multi-storey attendant, politely.

'Have you got the ticket, Baz?'

'Yeah, Gaz. You know I 'ave. I just found it.'

'Give it to me then, son. Here we are mate. Lousy weather ain't it?'

'Not too good, sir. Better later, I hear. That'll be twenty pence, please.'

'Here we go. Ta, mate.'

'Have a good day, sir.'

'We will, mate.'

The exit barrier was raised, and we spilled out on to Tolpuddle Gate. Then left on to High Street. The opposite direction to Comberton and home.

'Wot do ya fink, Gaz? Get us five grand for this beauty?'

'Maybe, Baz. These are the bee's knees.'

'Immac though, ain't it? Luvverly motor.'

'Yeah, luvverly.'

The air was thick with smoke. The Man Who Fenced Motors was drawing heavily on a huge Havana cigar, while the car thief called Gaz puffed away on a Capstan full strength. We were somewhere completely unknown to me. It wasn't Grevington, I knew that much. We had been on the road for too long. All I did know was we were under an old, dripping, closed-in railway arch, as I could hear the rumbling and clanking above me as the trains went about their business. Clearly, the place had been converted into a garage. Not one like the main agent where I was regularly serviced. There the floor shone and was spotless, and the mechanics were called technicians.

This place was filthy. Oil and spills of sawdust were spotted all over the floor. Grease was smeared on the walls and work-benches, and there wasn't a single window to be seen. Car innards were strewn everywhere. Conrods, pistons, coil springs, exhausts, starter motors, master cylinders. It was like a ferrous abattoir.

'Four grand,' offered the Man Who Fenced Motors, rolling the cigar between his podgy fingers.

'Five. It's worth it.'

'Four two fifty, tops. Hard to pass these on, Gaz. Not many around, see.'

'Four seven fifty dead, no less.'

'Four five. Take it or leave it. I've got other people to see, son.'

'OK, I'll take it. You drive a hard bargain, Bob.'

'Need to fink of me pension, son. Need to fink of me pension.' The Man Who Fenced Motors took a thick roll of banknotes out of the pocket of his greasy sheepskin coat, peeled off the required number in fifties, and carefully placed them in the grimy palms of the other man, one by one. The transaction took some time.

'See ya soon, Bob,' called Gaz as he pocketed the cash, slid through the door and disappeared into the enveloping gloom outside.

'OK, son. Next time bring me summat common, eh? Summat I can move easy?' the Man Who Fenced Motors shouted after him.

'Yeah, yeah.'

Once Gaz had departed the Man Who Fenced Motors laid a cold palm on my roof and gave me a gentle pat.

'Well, me old son, we've done well 'ere. Should get five and a half grand for this little beauty, no sweat. A good bargain. Yeah, a very good bargain.'

Satisfied with himself he glanced briefly around the gloomy place, walked over to the small door set within the larger semicircular doors, extinguished the lights and stepped out into the dark and unlit street beyond.

'Where are you from?' whispered an enquiring voice. 'Yes, you Mister Dolomite Sprint. Where are you from?'

'Coventry, originally,' I whispered back. 'But I now live in Comberton.'

'Comberton, eh? Very posh. I've been there,' floated another voice from the murkiness.

'Stole you, did he?' enquired another voice.

'I suppose so. It all happened rather quickly.'

'You suppose so? Have you never been stolen before? Not once since you were made?'

'No.'

'Blimey, you must have led a charmed life. Mind you, that may not last.'

'What do you mean?'

'The Treatment.'

'The Treatment?'

'Yes, the Treatment. That's what they do with cars they steal.'

'What's the Treatment?' I asked.

There was a sharp communal intake of air as I posed this question.

'Do you really want to know?'

'Yes, I do.'

'First, they pull off your number plates.'

'Ooooh!' chorused the voices.

'Then, they stick masking tape all over you.'

'Aaaagh!' chorused the voices.

'Then, they change your colour. All over.'

'Eeeeh!' chorused the voices.

'And if that's not enough, they then sell you to a dodgy dealer!'

'Yrrrgh!' chorused the voices.

I began to shiver. Nobody had ever talked to me about being stolen. It was one of those taboo subjects that was never mentioned in polite company. I'd heard rumours about what happened to stolen cars, but no car I knew had ever been stolen, so no car could tell the story of what really happens. Not in my neighbourhood, anyway.

The strange thing was that up to now I had rather enjoyed the experience. Roger, in the five years we had been together, had never, ever driven me like Gaz had, from the big multi-storey to wherever I was now. We had been through the entire repertoire: Foot-Flat-To-The-Floor, Round-The-Corners-On-Two-Wheels, Crashing-Through-The-Gears, Stamping-On-The-Brakes. My, had it been exhilarating! I had never, ever, felt so liberated in all my life.

My life. Where was it going now? Where would I end up next and what shame and suffering would I undergo? And I couldn't stop thinking about the Treatment. What an invasion of a body! I had always been red – I had no wish to be resprayed!

All fell silent. They were settling down for the evening to await the early morning return of the Man Who Fenced Motors and his Treatment Crew.

You could hear a pin drop. As I was nodding off with all sorts of wild imaginings flitting in and out of my restless sleep, I thought I did hear one drop. A scraping of metal against one of the big, semicircular doors followed by a much louder metallic crack on the outside. Then I heard mumbled voices as the inset door was forced open and a pencil-thin light from a torch was shone through the opening.

'Hurry up… we'll have to be quick.'

The torch beam danced around the cavernous space as if it had a life of its own. It quickly passed over a Ford Sierra, hovered over a Volvo 240, traced a locus around the cold, damp brick walls and passed silently across my windscreen, moved on, paused momentarily and then returned, pointing painfully at me like the concentrated pinprick of light an optician shines into a patient's eyes during an eye test.

'There. That one. The Sprint.'

That one? Me?

'That's the one we'll take. Do it.'

'OK. Easy.'

For the second time that day I felt another clammy, hot hand yank my door handle. Only on this occasion I didn't have to suffer the ignominy of having a cold, looped wire slipped over the top of my closed door. The Man Who Fenced Motors reckoned he had no need to fear theft from his premises. He was mistaken.

'Piece of cake. Someone's already wired this one.'

'I'll get the door. Quick now.'

Not for the first time that day I jumped as the wires were shorted forcing my starter motor to turn and springing my engine into life.

I was amazed. Not one attempted theft in five years and suddenly boom! Two in one day.

'Open the doors. Quietly now, we don't want anyone to hear us.'

'Hear us? No one lives anywhere near this dump.'

'OK, OK. Let's go.'

Another unknown pair of hands gripped my steering wheel and carefully eased me through the now open corrugated doors into the inky darkness beyond. Where, oh where was I going to end up next? Was I destined to face some fate worse than, or equally as worrying as the Treatment?

We began to gain speed and wound our way around blocks of silhouetted buildings until we came to a main road. Another one that I didn't recognise.

'Left here, then stop.' This voice was rather better spoken than my previous captors. There was hardly any trace of an accent. 'I'll go through it once more. Make sure you fully understand, all right?'

We pulled up at the side of the road.

'I'm listening.'

'We'll pick Jim up at the Fox and Hounds in fifteen minutes. He's got the gear with him. We'll then drive to Goldshine's Jewellers in Mount Pleasant Road. You drop us off, then park in the back of the Woolpack. Precisely twenty-five minutes after you've dropped us off, be back to pick us up. Not a minute sooner, and not a minute later. Then we'll ditch the car, split up, and meet next Tuesday in Marylebone Station by the news stand. That's all there is to it. Simple. Got it?'

'Got it.'

'Good.'

The word 'ditch' made me jump. This could be worse than the Treatment. Ditched? What exactly did 'ditched' mean? Was I literally to be driven into a ditch and left with my bodily fluids seeping into some stagnant and evil-smelling watercourse? Or did it mean something more diabolical still? I'd heard tales of cars being doused in petrol and set on fire in order to remove all traces of the thieves who'd stolen them. Imagine that – set on fire. Alive!

My day was getting a whole lot worse. I began to wish I was back in the warmth of the garage, protected from the outside world. Why was this happening to me?

We pulled away and before long joined a busy main road filled with an endless stream of cars. I tried to attract the attention of the others but to no avail. Their drivers were all too keen to reach wherever it was they were going, and on these derestricted roads the cars were hurrying along without a second thought. My luck was truly out. Worse, it was starting to rain. Heavily.

After fifteen minutes or so we turned off the arterial road into what appeared to be a small, quiet town. Quiet was why we turned off, I presumed. Pulling into a car park I could see an illuminated sign: Fox and Hounds.

A thin man in an oversized black raincoat was standing next to the sign, the light glistening on his oily back as he hunched down to protect himself from the rain. The driver pulled up next to him. My rear door was opened and the thin man slid into the back seat, a quick nod acknowledging his companions. No words were spoken. But there was a terrible smell of halitosis. (I knew this condition some drivers suffered was often brought on by anxiety.)

We started off again. The rain was getting worse by the minute, and my windscreen was beginning to mist up. This was another example of accountants penny-pinching and expecting drivers to cope with steamed-up windows. It was hard enough for me to keep my rear window clear ('Special Editions' often had rear windscreen heater elements), but I just didn't have the strength to clear all of my windows in such conditions and with three people breathing so heavily inside. I could hear the man in the back's rasping breath.

'OK, we're here. Pull over,' directed the well-spoken voice.

'I can't see a flaming thing, it's all steamed up,' complained the driver.

'Hurry up man!'

Bang!

Ow! That really hurt! The driver had misjudged the where-abouts of the kerb and my front nearside wheel mounted the pavement. It made my gearbox judder, I can tell you.

'Fucking hell!' screamed the black raincoat from the rear seat.

Bang! Another judder as we dropped down from the pavement on to the road again.

Silence.

My windows were so fogged with condensation by now that all three men were frantically wiping them with their coat sleeves to get their bearings.

'Shit!' hissed the black raincoat.

While toiling frantically to clear the torrents of water from my windscreen I hadn't been taking any notice of the road in front of me. Now I spotted two things. Firstly, we were parked on a double yellow line. Second, a police panda car with two policemen sitting inside was parked directly opposite.

The driver in his temporary blindness hadn't noticed the double yellow lines as he bounced me on and off the pavement. Which would have meant nothing if the two policeman hadn't been observing his antics.

I suppose you could call it luck, or destiny. It may have appeared to the cops that the driver might have been drinking and the episode with the kerb demonstrated a certain lack of control posing a danger to other road users. It may have been they were bored and were looking for an excuse to needle someone. Whatever it was, one of those policemen took it upon himself to think about introducing himself to my driver and must have informed his colleague. In unison, both policemen stepped out of the panda and slowly started to cross the road.

With hindsight, the three men sitting in me should have held their nerve. They hadn't committed any crime. (Although they had stolen me from a thief. Does thieving from a thief constitute a crime?) The two men in the front sat stock still, eyes averted from the oncoming officers.

The black coat in the back didn't. Cursing, he flung open the door, threw himself out on to the pavement and streaked off into the night. His action triggered panic in the other two, who followed suit.

As we all know, this kind of behaviour is like a red rag to the constabulary bull. They hared off after the two men, one blowing his whistle and the other shouting into his walkie-talkie.

So, there I was. Doors wide open, rain pouring down, in a strange place and totally exhausted.

'Well, well, m'lad. What have you been up to?'

I looked across the road to where the voice came from. It was the panda car.

Now you may not know this, but on the whole we cars are much more caring and considerate than our drivers usually are. There was sympathy in the panda car's voice. He could see from my condition that I was not the kind of car that normally associated with the criminal classes. From the forlorn look in my headlights I think he had already pieced together what had been happening to me.

'You've been stolen, haven't you?'

'Twice. In one day.'

'My Lord! Twice in one day! I don't think I've ever come across that before.'

I explained my story to him, parked there that wet, miserable night.

Early the next day after spending a night in the police compound, I was relieved to see the arrival of Roger. He didn't notice, but my grille was shining. Looking me all over to make sure I was all right, he patted me lovingly on my front wing before driving me home. Rain from the previous night had given way to a bright, sunny day, and Roger decided to give me a lovely wash, wax and polish to clear the grime of the previous evening.

I never did know what happened to the three men. Nor to the Man Who Fenced Motors. Nor to Gaz and Baz. I didn't want to, either. I was back in safe hands.

Magda (1984)

It all started one gloriously sunny morning in June. Roger had been instructed to take Daisy for a walk along the towpath of the local canal. Daisy was a recent acquisition of Sylvia's, much to the unspoken annoyance of Roger, who deep down detested dogs. As usual, however, Sylvia got her way and he now found himself shambling along behind a rather excitable springer spaniel.

Perhaps he should have put his foot down, but the heart-breaking memories of her inability to have a baby had again prevented him from doing so. Every time their friends with growing children expressed the joys of parenthood, he saw how much it broke Sylvia's heart knowing she would always remain childless. In his own mind he'd come to terms with the fact that he was destined never to be a father, but instead the husband of a pet collector. First it was Henry and now this blasted dog.

Of course, over the past few years the horse had been a great comfort and diversion for Sylvia who, every morning without fail, continued to attend to his needs at the stables. But even Roger and Henry weren't enough. She craved for the companionship of an animal at home. He knew the springer was another child substitute.

'What a beautiful dog. What's her name?' Roger was shaken out of his cogitating by the unexpected question. He looked behind him to see a girl with a large black Labrador lolling on a lead she held in her hand.

'Down, Titan. Sit!' The big dog sat back on its haunches immediately at the sound of the girl's command. Not so with Daisy. She rushed forward to sniff at the sitting dog, forcing Roger to pull back hard on her lead.

'Whoa, whoa!' shouted Roger, using all his strength to drag Daisy away from the other dog. 'Whoa, whoa there!'

This triggered a bout of giggling from the girl.

'Sorry,' she apologised, covering her mouth with her hand,

but to no avail. She continued to giggle uncontrollably.

'Is something the matter?' asked Roger, putting on a superior tone of voice, at the same time sneakily scrutinising himself to see what might be the cause of her amusement. No, a quick inspection revealed that his flies were zipped up.

'No, no… it's just…'

'Just what?'

'The way you said "whoa", as if you were reining in a mad horse.' The fits of giggling began again. 'Sorry, I just can't help it. It just sounds so, well… stiff.'

'I'm not surprised,' snorted Roger, still straining to control the excitable Daisy. 'I haven't a clue how to handle dogs. Never had one before.' Shrugging his shoulders he took in the appearance of the amused girl in front of him. He guessed she would be in her very early twenties, tall and slim. However, it was her clothes and unusual jewellery that struck him most.

From head to toe she was clothed completely in black. Nowhere did another colour break the dark expanse. She wore a pair of heavy black workman's boots, and he'd never seen a female wearing such boots before. Then he studied the jewellery she had on. It was chunky and in complete contrast to the stereotypical adornments that he imagined all women wore, given his knowledge of Sylvia's own jewellery box and the women at work. And her hair! It stuck straight out from her head at all angles like Dennis the Menace in the cartoons he'd been so fond of as a boy. He didn't think he'd ever seen such an unusual sight. Unusual, but not unattractive. Decidedly different, though.

Roger realised he was now staring rudely at the girl instead of concentrating on getting Daisy under control.

'Here, let me.' The girl, who by now had stopped her giggling, stepped over to Roger and gently took the lead from his hand. Taking a rolled-up newspaper from out of her shoulder bag she rapped Daisy sharply on the nose – just once. The startled dog yelped but the rap had the immediate effect of calming her down and she turned away and slunk off to hide behind Roger's legs. Handing the lead back to Roger, the girl replaced the rolled-up newspaper in her bag.

'I think your dog needs a little discipline,' she advised.

'Otherwise I guarantee your life will become a misery. You have to show her who's boss, you know. Come Titan. Heel!' Off she went with the big dog trailing behind her.

As he continued on his walk with Daisy skulking beside him he couldn't help thinking of what had just happened. Reflecting on how his life had been dominated by females – first his mother, then his wife, and now – for God's sake – her dog, he wondered at approaching forty years of age how many more would treat him like an infant. Even the girl on the towpath had had to show him how to control Daisy, as if he were clueless on the subject – which he was.

'That's it,' he muttered to himself. 'I'm going to take things into my own hands. They all think I'm helpless. Well, no more. I'm going to do something about it.'

Quite what, he didn't know.

'Heel! Heel! Bloody stupid dog!'

It was exactly one week after he bumped into the girl that Roger was out for a walk with Daisy on the same canal towpath. Every day since that chance meeting he'd walked the dog, determined to control the animal and make her obedient to his commands. Copying the girl, he'd rolled up a newspaper with the intention of using it if the dog misbehaved – which he assumed she wouldn't after her last chastisement. How wrong that assumption was. On the very next day the dog started to get up to her old tricks – barking loudly at anyone she saw, tugging Roger with all her might, and jumping up at any passers-by. Thinking he'd show her who was the boss, Roger had produced the rolled up paper and shown it to the animal, which responded by baring her teeth at him and snapping at his trouser leg. Luckily she failed to find flesh and simply shredded the turn-up of his trousers. Roger let go of the lead in surprise, allowing Daisy to sprint off down the towpath barking like mad at everything in sight. It had taken him a further three quarters of an hour to catch up with her, and only then because her lead had snagged a bollard which stuck up like a jagged tooth at one of the moorings. By now she was worn out and, growling all the way home, followed Roger as far away from him as the lead would allow.

'Still having trouble?' asked a voice from behind him. He turned round to see the same girl, but this time she was walking a pony-size mastiff that was loping along obediently beside her. At the sound of her voice the most remarkable change came over Daisy. She sank to the ground, put her head between her front paws and looked up at the girl dressed all in black.

'Er, no,' lied Roger. 'She's just a bit frisky today.'

'And what about the other day when she was causing havoc?' accused the girl.

'She was having a bad day,' answered Roger, defensively.

'Another one?'

'She just wanted a run, that's all. She's full of energy.' Roger shrugged his shoulders.

'You can't manage her. I saw panic written all over your face.'

'OK, OK. I tried your trick with the newspaper. It didn't work.'

'It's not a trick, and you shouldn't have hit her. That was wrong,' scolded the girl.

'You did it, and it worked for you.'

'That's because she doesn't know me. She knows you – and she knows you're weak. I mean, weak as far as she's concerned. They're just like people, you know. Dogs know what they can and can't get away with. They're really quite clever.'

'How do you know?' asked Roger, who was being eyeballed by the mastiff. He was sure the big dog had a knowing look on its face.

'I'm a professional dog trainer. It's what I do. And just in case you're wondering I'm also a punk, and proud of it.' She glared defiantly at Roger.

'I see.' Eyeing her warily, he racked his brain without success to remember what a punk might be, and wasn't sure if it was a good or a bad thing. She'd confronted the wrong person, however. Roger Bunting hadn't a clue what a punk was. The heady years of the Sex Pistols, the Clash, and others had passed him by. He preferred the classical composers.

'My advice to you would be to get some professional help. You'll never cure that dog of its naughtiness otherwise.' She continued to glare at him.

Roger took stock of the situation. He could either continue with the status quo, making his dog-walking days a misery. He could tell Sylvia to 'walk the bloody dog yourself', which would really be going out on a limb. Or he could take the girl's advice and get some professional help. No contest really.

'OK, I admit I do need help with the dog. Would you be prepared to take her away and teach her some manners? I'll pay, of course, seeing as how you make your living at it. What do you say?'

The girl slowly shook her head from side to side.

'It doesn't work like that. It's not up to me. You have to do the work. I show you how to go about it. But at the end of the day she has to learn how to respect you – not me. And I'm not sure whether I have any time at the moment. I'm very busy with my other clients. Up, Sultan! Let's go!' The mastiff sprang to its feet, still staring at Roger, and in one swift movement the girl and dog were striding away from him down the towpath.

Daisy jumped up, almost pulling Roger over, and started barking with all her might.

During the next fortnight the weather degenerated into one of those typically irritating spells that Britain suffers. Days were grey, chilly and relentlessly drizzly. The Buntings, not being of an outdoors inclination, hunkered down in the evenings after work in the warmth and snugness of their cosy home. This didn't suit Daisy, who developed a nasty little habit of chewing just about everything she could get her canine teeth into.

'You'll have to take her for a decent walk, darling. Five times round the garden just isn't good enough. All this chewing, I think it must be a boredom thing.' Sylvia struggled to wrest yet another of her slippers from the dog's mouth. Daisy was clearly enjoying the tug of war.

'But it's pouring down,' complained Roger.

Daisy's tail was now wagging to and fro like a metronome on steroids. She wasn't going to let go of the slipper at any cost. Oh, no she really liked this new game. Not so Sylvia. Tired with the ceaseless jerking of her hand she let go of the slipper at precisely the moment Daisy's head pulled back in expectation of an increased resistance.

The startled animal shot backwards, crashing into a coffee table and scattering its contents all over the lounge carpet. Yelping loudly she then streaked around the lounge strewing ornaments, books and papers all over the place.

'That's it!' screamed Sylvia. 'Roger, take her out for a walk! Now!'

Roger stood up to get his overcoat.

There wasn't a soul in sight. No wonder, he thought, on such a miserable evening. Rain was pelting down like stair rods and making a bass drumming on the surface of the canal. All along the sodden towpath were wide puddles which he gingerly tried to avoid. He might as well not have bothered, as the skittish Daisy seemed to delight in jumping up and down in them, soaking his trousers, shoes, and socks in the process.

Whether it was because the lead was wet, or a temporary loss of concentration he would never be quite sure. Daisy unexpectedly made one of her dashes and the lead flew out of Roger's hand. The dog's pent-up energy was now released and she streaked off at high speed down the towpath, barking madly with the elation of being free.

'God no, not again,' muttered Roger to himself. He recalled the recent occurrence when Daisy had caused pandemonium and the subsequent chastisement he had received from that girl in black. Wearily he resigned himself to getting absolutely drenched in his quest to retrieve Sylvia's errant pet. Gripping his overcoat collar tightly around his neck and shoving his now leadless hand deep into his pocket, he peered through the lashing rain to see if he could see the dog ahead of him, but it was impossible to see further than fifty feet through the watery curtain obscuring the landscape.

He found her quicker than he expected. A series of squeals, increasing in intensity, reached him through the blurriness of the downpour, accompanied by a deep and throaty roar. As he started to run towards the sounds visibility improved marginally and he was able to make out two indistinct shapes at the side of the towpath. One, dark and squat, was tossing a much less substantial brown and white form around in the air as if it were a rag doll. Within twenty feet now, Roger could clearly see that a large

Doberman had Daisy by the throat and was on the verge of pinning her to the ground.

'Hoi, stoppit!' he screeched at the assailant while waving his arms wildly in the air. 'Get off her, you brute! Go!'

At first the dog took no notice, but it changed its mind when it saw a wild-looking form rushing towards it, arms waving like a windmill's sails spinning in a force 10. Growling once, as if to complain of being denied its prize, it unlocked its jaws from Daisy's throat and slinked off into the field that abutted the towpath.

Kneeling down to where Daisy lay, Roger could hear the poor animal whimpering with fright, shocked by the mugging she'd just received. Her neck and back were covered in blood, though on quick inspection no profuse bleeding was obvious. Sliding both arms under the body Roger lifted the dog off the soaking gravel and retraced his steps homeward.

On his return to Coombe View Roger was given a thorough marital rollocking when Sylvia saw the state of her beloved new pet.

This must be the right address, he thought. It had been the only one in the local telephone directory offering such a service. The property was a semi-detached bungalow on the edge of Comberton, close to Milverton Road. His assumption proved correct when he heard the barking of several dogs responding to the chime as he pressed the doorbell.

A large, young man with a shaven head, and sporting a huge chrome earring in his left ear, opened the door.

'Yes, mate?' asked the young man.

'Is this the right address for the Rosemount Dog Training School?' Roger enquired, not sure whether perhaps he had come to the right place after all.

'Yes, mate. Wait there.' Shaven head shut the door and Roger heard him shuffle off away down what must have been the hallway. He then shouted something which Roger couldn't make out. The shout was answered by a female voice. Slowly, the front door opened and the girl in black stood before him, hands on hips.

'I heard about your dog,' she said. 'Rather nasty, wasn't it?'

'Yes, it was. Who told you?'

'John Anderson.'

'John Anderson?' Roger thought hard to put a face to the name. 'Should I know him?'

'You should. He's the vet who stitched your dog up. He's also my father. What do you want? I'm very busy.'

'I need your help, please. With the dog training. I'm at my wits' end.'

'Before you get her killed, you mean?'

'Yes. Before I get her killed,' admitted Roger, feeling very humble.

This was the seventh session Daisy and Roger had attended. Over the past five weeks the dog's attitude toward its master had improved beyond belief. Roger had even grown to like the animal. No longer were the towpath walks something to dread; a one-sided battle which Daisy was always going to win. No longer did she strain at the lead, or bark at the ducks or other dogs. No more jumping up excitedly at people she encountered. Magda had performed miracles.

Magda. The girl in black. The vet's daughter. The punk.

Magda was fantastic with dogs. It was as if she could speak their language. She never had any problem with mischievousness after a dog's second or third session. No matter what dog she was given to train – and the yappy little ones were far worse than the Great Danes, Alsatians, Dobermans, and wolf hounds – they were as meek as lambs when she'd finished with them. It must have been a natural gift. She helped Roger to work with Daisy and gain the dog's respect. Step by step some of Magda's technique was miraculously transferred to Roger. He was very impressed.

He also noticed that underneath all the gloomy appearance Magda was a lovely-looking girl, tall and slim with a fine bone structure, smooth sallow skin, and a wicked grin when she wanted to display it. He wondered what she would be like if she ever shed the punk uniform and those big boots for something a little more feminine. The thought intrigued him. She also had much more about her than just an ability with dogs. Roger discovered she had a brain and could engage him on any subject he chose. More than that, she knew far more about the world around him than he'd garnered in his forty years. It came as a surprise to him at the end of the seventh session when she asked him if he'd ever been to see a punk band, and he had to admit he didn't know what a punk band was. So she explained to him the social origins of the punk movement – why it had come about, what its purpose was, what it hoped to achieve. Roger listened attentively to the way she explained it, and some of the rationale made sense to him. He recognised his upbringing had been very sheltered and wondered if something momentous had passed him by completely during his teenage years. She told him why she dressed as she did (to shock people), who the large man with the bald head was (her brother Jake – another punk) and the attitude of her father to her and Jake's 'punkiness' (very liberal; he himself had been the founder of a skiffle group in the early fifties when skiffle was frowned upon by the establishment).

She was so refreshing in comparison with Sylvia and his somewhat narrow-minded, money-focused friends, and in a strange way Roger found her to be, well, quite magnetic.

'Seeing as how you've never been to one would you like to go to a punk gig, Roger?' she asked him at the end of their latest session. 'I think you might even enjoy it.'

Roger's brow creased. This wouldn't go down well at home. Agreeing to a strangely attired young woman asking him to go to a punk rock concert would not be taken as the act of a sane man. The Spanish Inquisition would be a picnic in comparison to the grilling he would get from Sylvia. Then he thought of the promise he'd made to himself while walking with an uncontrollable Daisy on the towpath and the self-loathing for his own helplessness in the presence of strong females. There was no need to consider the answer. This was his chance to make a stand.

'Why not? I think I would.'

Of course, he wouldn't tell Sylvia.

It must have awoken a dormant gene. Two hours of shouting, screaming, sweating with what? Excitement? Yes, excitement. That was the only word that could describe how Roger felt that evening. Here was a man whom the sixties had ignored. While he and his cronies were immersed in war-gaming and chess, the world turned. Several times. They'd missed Lonnie Donegan, Mersey sound, the Beatles, flower power, Tamla, the Monkees and heavy metal. By the time Roger was in his early twenties he'd been bypassed by a musical revolution without realising it. In his late twenties and thirties his contemporary musical ignorance continued. He had become a cultural dinosaur.

Until now.

At first he didn't know what the hell he was doing there. He'd been fearful that he'd stand out like a sore thumb. Good old, conservative, prematurely middle-aged Roger Bunting. A quiet, unassuming, and henpecked accountant. He needn't have worried. There were men and women of all ages in the audience. Quite why this was he couldn't figure out, as his research indicated that punk was essentially a platform for teenage rebellion in its heyday in the mid-seventies. Nowadays though, Magda informed him, all that had changed. Punk had mellowed and consequently attracted a much broader parish of followers. You just had to like the music. Simple.

Roger did. The jarring music struck a chord somewhere deep down in his ossified consciousness. Within thirty minutes of the warm-up band starting (Spike My Pint from Lower Mortcombe) he was swaying, clapping and shouting with the throng around him, all traces of self-consciousness completely erased. He even joined hands with complete strangers. The alcohol may have helped things along a little, too. Many of the audience had secreted small bottles or flasks on their persons, and Jake was no exception. From time to time he took out a silver hip flask and passed it to Roger and Magda. Carried away in the hysteria, Roger took several deep swigs during the concert.

At the end of the evening Jake excused himself in order to 'see Rod about some business'. Winking at Roger and kissing his sister on the cheek he left them in Waverton village hall's car park.

'What did you think?' asked Magda.

'Great. My ears are still buzzing. It was really good.'

'What will you tell you wife?' she asked, a wicked grin appearing on her face.

Roger froze. He'd lied to Sylvia that he would be meeting with a client to discuss some tricky points on their tax return. As the client wouldn't have an opportunity to spare the time during the day, the meeting needed to be outside normal working hours. She'd accepted this without question during this busy time of year when many companies prepared their yearly accounts.

'How do you know I'm married?' asked Roger, stalling for time.

'Oh come on, Roger. It's written through you like a stick of Blackpool rock. If I cut your head off it'd be inscribed in a circle around your neck – Married Man. Plus the fact that your wedding ring gives it away,' she giggled. There was something in that giggle that Roger found very appealing.

'OK. I am married. I'll say I was out with—'

'One of your clients?' she finished his sentence for him.

'Yes. One of my clients.'

'Then you'll have to say the client was female.' Magda slid the slim fingers of her left hand around Roger's sweating neck and drew his head close to hers. Closing her eyes she pressed her full lips against his mouth and held them there.

Something needed to escape in Roger. It was bubbling up from deep down inside and desperately trying to get to the surface. Like an experienced diver, the 'something' knew better than to rush skywards, otherwise it would suffer terrible pain from the 'bends'. But it was determined to break out of its watery gaol and was inexorably committed to making the journey. It wouldn't be stopped.

The embrace with Magda had been a defining moment. He found himself unable to do that which his mind told him he should have done. Push her away, tell her not to be silly, chastise her for her forwardness. Any one of a dozen reactions which would have been embarrassing for one or the other, or both of them, but it would have re-established the boundaries in their relationship and ultimately been locked away as a skeleton in each of their personal cupboards.

He was definitely intrigued by Magda. Magda was very different. She was a free spirit, not dictated to by time or habit.

She did what she wanted to do, and hang what anyone thought. Magda stood out from other women in Roger's life. She asked him for his advice, valued his opinions, and didn't put him down if she thought differently.

But it wasn't lust or passion that was bubbling up deep inside Roger.

The late summer sun was gently and slowly setting over the rolling hills of Comberton when Roger pulled me up on the drive. There was no sign of anyone at home. Locking my doors he fumbled for his keys, opened the front door to the house and disappeared inside.

It was the third time he had been out with Magda and Jake. The third time he had invented a fictitious meeting with a client. It couldn't continue. He would have to come clean with Sylvia. Then it would be out in the open and the air would be cleared. There would be some explaining to do of course, but why should that worry him? There was no feeling of guilt on his part. He never questioned Sylvia when she had a night out visiting her friend Carole. It was a matter simply of choosing the right moment.

Tonight would be as good a time as any to tell her.

At the precise moment Roger was parking me on the drive, in the well-lit hallway of a spacious and secluded house situated in the stockbroker belt of Barchester, a good-looking woman was studying herself in a gilded mirror and applying a fresh coat of bright crimson lipstick to a puckered mouth. After dabbing at the corners with a tissue, she smoothed her rich mane of hair with a beautifully manicured hand, straightened the seams of her pencil skirt and slowly put on her camel-coloured coat.

She didn't feel good about the deception and was still surprised at how easy it had been to do. That was so typical of men. When they were in the early stages of a relationship they were all over you. Interested in everything about you. Thoughts, feelings, clothes, friends, interests. Once they had you in their little trap their interest soon waned. Her deceit had been possible thanks to Carole, a fictitious 'old school friend' whom he had never met and would never meet. That was a very clever piece of invention on her part, and one he had accepted without question.

'Have a good time at Carole's. I'll see you later. Call me if you have any problems with the train,' was all he ever said. If only he'd been more prying it would probably never have happened. Or would it? Would she have taken the man as her lover anyway?

She was happily married, of course she was. Her husband was a good man. Diligent, faithful, reliable, a good provider. Being happily married, however, hadn't helped her with the moods of darkest gloom to which she was prone; particularly after the strong recommendation from her obstetrician not to try any more for children. The doctor's counsel had been that they should consider adoption as the best course. She had received the same advice from her aunt. There was no way she was going to consider adoption. Absolutely no way.

The affair had taken some time to develop. Her lover was quite a few years older than her; just turned fifty, tallish, with a military bearing. The man dressed immaculately and was blessed with an immense amount of charm, and a colossal amount of money.

'We'd best be going, my love, otherwise you'll miss your train,' whispered the man in the woman's ear, as he ran the tip of his finger down the curve of her back.

'Oh, Conrad, I always feel so guilty when I get home. Perhaps we should just come clean with Roger and get everything out in the open.'

'Now why would you want to do that, my love? You have a perfectly good marriage to a good man who would do anything for you. Yes, you do like a frisson of excitement in your life – as do I – which is why we have such a good thing going. No strings attached. The way we both like it.'

'He's changed recently.' She turned to face him.

'Changed? In what way?'

'I think he suspects there may be something going on. He's become, well, more assertive.'

'Are you sure you're not imagining it? After all, it's Roger we're talking about here.'

'Well, whatever it is, he's not the same as he was. Maybe he's having an affair?'

At this Conrad burst into laughter. 'Oh come on Sylvia, this is your husband we're talking about. He's like a faithful hound. I don't think you need ever be worried on that score. Come along, we'd best be going.'

'Hello, darling,' greeted Sylvia as she climbed in me after coming out of the station.

'Hello, darling,' he responded mechanically, giving her a peck on the cheek. 'How's Carole?'

'She's fine. Never better,' answered Sylvia.

'Any interesting gossip?'

'Not really. If there was, would you be interested?'

'Not really.'

The Buntings remained silent for the rest of the journey home. Both put the silence down to tiredness after a long and busy day.

As Roger headed for the kitchen Sylvia slipped off her coat and draped it over the back of a chair in the lounge. Kicking her shoes off and digging her toes into the deep, soft pile of the cream Wilton carpet, she sank into the comfort of the leather settee and tucked her long legs beneath her. It was good to be home. Why, oh why, had she ever started the clandestine affair with Conrad, she wondered.

It had been going on for two years now. Initially there was no physical attraction, just another blossoming friendship. Over time though, in a myriad of small ways, she began to feel a dangerously exciting sexual attraction for the man. She couldn't quite put her finger on what it was that made her feel like a moth caught in a candle flame in his presence. Was it his confidence, his wealth, his vitality, his power, or something much deeper? Maybe, like her father, he had a stronger will than her and she found this irresistible. Whatever it was, the relationship had gone far beyond the harmless flirting that it should have been. What made her feel really guilty was the invented deception of Carole in order to escape the house every Tuesday evening. The idea wasn't even Conrad's, so she couldn't lay the blame at his feet. It was fairly and squarely with her.

'How was your meeting?' enquired Sylvia.

'Oh, rather dull. Nothing much to report on. Would you like some supper?'

'A glass of milk and a digestive biscuit would be good, thanks.'

Of late her conscience was beginning to trouble her, like a maggot gnawing away in the nourishing depths of an apple. The last couple of visits to see Conrad had been decidedly uncomfortable. Tonight they hadn't made love, and had passed the evening engaged in small talk about nothing in particular. She wondered if he'd detected the beginnings of a rift in their relationship and she was relieved when it was time for her to leave.

'One glass of milk and a biscuit coming up.' Roger set the glass and plate down on the coffee table in front of her. Settling himself down into his favourite armchair, he rested his elbows on the arms, steepled his fingers and rested his chin on them. It was not a relaxed position.

Neither of them spoke. Sylvia chewed absently on her biscuit and took the occasional sip from the glass. She appeared to be unaware of Roger, as if her mind were elsewhere.

Troubled by the silence Roger began to fidget, turning this way and then that in his chair. Under normal circumstances he would have received a reprimand from Sylvia, usually telling him to 'Sit still, darling. You're making me nervous.' It hadn't taken her long to familiarise herself with his habits and she knew when he had a problem or worry he involuntarily fiddled. Tonight she didn't even notice. Roger continued to fidget.

After ten minutes the squirming ceased. Roger couldn't stand it any longer. For several weeks this had been building up and it was time to come clean. He settled back in his chair and started to drum on the arms with his fingers, tapping a metronomic beat with his right foot on the carpet. No, it was no good. No matter the consequences, this had to be done. Now.

Pushing himself up from the chair he shuffled across the room and stood directly in front of the fireplace. Stuffing his hands into his pockets he began to gently sway back and forth, rocking on the heels of his slippers.

'Sylvia. There's something I need to talk to you about.'

It was one of the rare times since they'd been married that he'd addressed her using her full name. Normally it was either

'Sylv', or 'darling'. For a second she didn't respond. Then she looked up at him.

'Whatever is the matter, darling? Did something happen in your meeting this evening?'

'No, it's nothing to do with my client. Well, that's not quite true. It is something to do with my client. In a way. On the other hand perhaps it isn't…'

'You're not making sense.'

'Fact is I wasn't with a client this evening.'

'Oh.' She uncurled her legs form under her, put the glass down on the table, smoothed her skirt and sat upright. She could feel her pulse quicken slightly. Did he know? Perhaps he's known for some time and said nothing? Did he keep quiet expecting that the cuckolding would fade away, a temporary fascination? He wasn't naive. Of course he knew. He was just too polite to say. God, I knew it would only be a matter of time. Why, oh why had I been so stupid to have encouraged the bloody affair?

'Look, darling—' she started, deciding to own up to the liaison before any accusations started flying.

'Please, Sylvia, don't interrupt me. I need to have this out.'

Sylvia felt a cold shiver race down her spine, and unconsciously took a draft from the glass of milk.

'I didn't see my client this evening. In fact, I haven't seen any of my clients in the evening for some time now. I've been doing something else.' Taking his hands out of his pockets he crossed his arms and looked her directly in the eye.

Oh, Christ. He's been following me. He knows where 'Carole' is supposed to live. It wouldn't take much effort for him to drive round the area, make some discreet enquiries and perhaps discover nobody knew a 'Carole'. Or maybe he suspected Conrad (perhaps her behaviour in his company had given her away) and had driven straight to Conrad's house. Roger's suspicions would be confirmed when he saw them arriving in the Aston after picking her up at the railway station.

'You know Magda…' he continued.

'Magda? Is that the girl who does the dog training?' she asked, a deep frown creasing her forehead as she recalled who the unusual name belonged to.

'Yes, that's her. Well I've been meeting up with her while you've been at Carole's,' he blurted out.

Sylvia felt her heart skip a beat. Had she misheard? Did he say he'd been meeting the girl who trained Daisy? While she was with Conrad? What in heaven's name was he going on about?

'I'm sorry Roger, I don't understand.'

'Please listen to me. It's important. You know I've been taking Daisy to dog training lessons with Magda? Well, we got to talking about punk rock, something I confess I'd never heard of. To cut a long story short she persuaded me to go and see a punk band performing at Waverton village hall. At first I was rather reluctant but I thought, why not? Anyway, I went with her and her brother Jake, and I found it to be… well, exhilarating. She asked me if I wanted to go again and I said yes.' At this point he thought it best not to mention the long and lingering – and only – kiss that Magda had given him after that first outing. 'That's where I've been every Tuesday for the past three weeks. Listening to live punk music.'

'Punk music? You've been going to listen to punk music? Are you feeling all right, Roger?'

There was something about him this evening. Had he been nipping at the whisky? It would be a first if he had. No, it wasn't that. He was perfectly lucid. She thought about it and it gradually dawned on her. His attitude. That was it. He was more forceful. Not like the husband she'd known for the past eight years.

'Never better, Sylvia. And I'm going to continue going there, as I really enjoy it.'

Thoughts were racing through Sylvia's head. He didn't have a clue about Conrad and her after all. She felt relief welling up inside. It was time to go on the offensive.

'Don't be so ridiculous, Roger! You're a middle-aged man for heaven's sake! All those dirty, noisy, drug-taking, low-class people? You want to be associated with them? Are you out of your mind?'

If he did stray into an argument with Sylvia, Roger would usually say nothing and silently bite his lip. Not that there were many arguments. He usually buckled at the first sign of any disagreement. This night was to reveal a different Roger Bunting.

Uncrossing his arms and shaking his head slowly from side to side, Roger walked around the coffee table and sat down next to her, their knees almost touching. Staring her straight in the eye without blinking he continued.

'Sylvia, do you know, all my life I've done what other people have told me to do? My grandmother, my mother, my bosses... now even my wife. All because everyone knows "good old Roger" won't embarrass himself by arguing with them. So they take advantage of me. I've put up with it for more damn years than I care to remember. And you know what? Over the past few weeks I've decided I've just about had enough. I will continue to go out on a Tuesday evening, whether you damn well like it or not.'

There was a threatening edge in his tone. Roger had crossed the Rubicon.

For the first time in her marriage she knew it would not be wise to argue.

'I can't continue with the lie, Conrad. I just can't. It's killing me.'

It was the week after Roger had laid the law down. Carrying on with the deception, she was again visiting the fictitious Carole. Just the mention of the name made her feel remorse. It pushed down on her and squeezed her pungent guilt out of the pores of her body like a garlic press. However was she going to extricate herself from this?

If she could, how would Carole suddenly disappear? Wrestling to find a solution was giving her indigestion and sleepless nights. Sylvia was not used to not having the answer.

'It's time to bring this to an end.'

He knew it was coming. He'd known for several weeks. Besides, the thrill had been in the hunt. Once the quarry was trapped he'd begun to lose interest, as he always did. The chase had taken some time, mind you. She hadn't been an easy prey. But she'd certainly been a worthwhile one.

But there was his ego to consider.

'Hey, listen. You're the one who's married. I didn't ask you to seduce me.' There was a touch of spite in Conrad's voice.

'I'm not so sure about who seduced whom. I think it was fifty–fifty.'

'Well, you wanted an affair, didn't you?'

'At the time, yes. I did.'

'And now?'

Sylvia took a deep breath.

'And now I don't.'

'So where does that leave me?'

Considering her answer very carefully, Sylvia looked the stylish man in front of her straight in the eye.

'Single, I'm afraid.'

'You know, Sylvia, that does have its attractions. There are many women who would give their all to be in your position. It's a pity, but it's no great loss. Of course, you do realise that this will make our social meetings a little awkward.'

She nodded, half knowing what was to follow.

'So you may find that Roger and yourself don't receive many invitations to Regis Hall in future.'

The Dordogne (1990)

In August 1990 Sylvia's Aunt June passed away in New Zealand after a short period of illness leaving her niece a not insubstantial sum of money in her will. Not as much as she left to the local cat's home mind you, but a tidy amount all the same. Maybe the money was left to assuage Aunt June's guilt at abandoning Sylvia and her sisters when they needed her most. Maybe it was because there was simply no one else to leave the money to. Her beloved Lance had passed away the year before, leaving June absolutely distraught. A victim of his own success, Lance had literally become tumescent with excessive consumption of fine wines and rich foods. When this was coupled with a sedentary lifestyle and a habit of chain-smoking endless packets of cigarettes, his bloated and corpulent body suffered a massive, fatal heart attack early one morning as he was taking his daily shower.

By now I was approaching my fifteenth birthday, which always just followed Roger and Sylvia's summer holidays. I admit it niggled me a little that I'd seen very little of the world in all those years, as I felt as sprightly as ever. Barring the annual pilgrimage to Scarborough I seldom travelled beyond the boundaries of the county. The Citroën belonging to our next-door neighbour Lawrence was much more fortunate. He'd visited his homeland three times in the past five years.

'Ah, mon ami, eet's such a fantastic experience to travel, especially to such a beautiful country as la France. Much less traffic zan 'ere. And ze contreeside… ah, eet's so magnifique. You must get zem to take you zere sometime.'

'I think that would be wishful thinking, Henri. Roger and Sylvia aren't exactly what you would call adventurous. Not in the least.'

'Zat's a great pity, mon cher. You would love la France. So varied, so hypnoteeq, so magnifique. I am so 'appy that Lawrence chooses to take me back zere every so often. Eet's so… 'ow you say… refreshing.'

Right at this moment refreshing would be good. The country had endured a terrible winter and spring with heavy and incessant rainfall over much of the South East and South West, which continued for days on end. Everyone's spirits had been dampened and the situation hadn't been helped by the poor economic trough the country had once more stuffed its snout into.

By the spring, people felt restless and thoughts of escaping to holidays in the sun were on everyone's mind. Even if Scarborough wasn't exactly a tropical haven or sun trap it felt at least as if a malaise was being left behind.

'Scarborough soon, eh mon brave?' enquired Henri.

'Where else?' I answered, not letting my imagination drift and dwell on all those unvisited and enchanting places.

'You know darling, I really do feel like doing something different this year. Rather than go to Scarborough, why don't we throw all caution to the wind and do something really different?' Sylvia was evidently in a good mood. It might have been something to do with the nice wad of money left by the maiden aunt which was already earmarked for a new suite, a kitchen makeover, four or five 'absolutely necessary' new outfits, a replacement for an ageing fridge... and oh, of course... a new suit for Roger. After all that there would still be a significant sum to tuck away into savings.

'I was thinking we might take the plunge and go a little further than Scarborough this year. Somewhere romantic.'

'What about Newquay?' suggested Roger.

'Oh, darling, you are so small-minded! I was thinking romantic, not aquatic! No, I've been doing some research and all the right people are taking their holidays in France this season.' (Sylvia was much attuned to what the 'right people' were doing.)

'France? But that's miles away. How in heaven's name would we get there?'

'By car of course! That's how everyone does it these days. We could drive to Portsmouth and take the ferry to Caen. We'd be in France in no time at all and could then take a leisurely drive down to our final destination – the Dordogne.' (Sylvia, who loved French at school, had never had the opportunity to visit France once the family misfortune struck.)

'Where?'

'The Dordogne. Listen to this.' She quickly fumbled in the magazine rack, took out a glossy brochure and turned to the page she'd saved with a bookmark – courtesy of Scarborough Castle.

' "The Dordogne is a beautiful region of south-west France between the Loire valley and the High Pyrenees named after the magnificent river that runs through it. However, locally it is known as the Périgord. This dates back to the time when the area was inhabited by the Gauls. There were four tribes living here and the name for 'four tribes' in the Gaulish language was 'Petrocore', which after a few hundred years became the Périgord and its inhabitants became the Périgordin. To confuse things further there are four Périgords in the Dordogne. The 'Périgord Verte' (Green Périgord) with its main town of Nontron, offers a greenery of verdant growth and valleys in a region crossed by a myriad of rivers and streams. The 'Périgord Blanc' (White Périgord) situated around the region's capital of Périgueux, is a region of limestone plateaux, wide valleys and rolling meadows. The 'Périgord Pourpre' (Purple Périgord) with its capital of Bergerac (the home of Cyrano), is the wine region, with full-bodied reds and sweet white Monbazilacs. The 'Périgord Noir' of Sarlat overlooks the valleys of the Vézère and the Dordogne, where the woods of oak and pine give it its name." Isn't that just incredible?'

'Yes, but it's not Scarborough, is it, darling? We always go to Scarborough. We had our honeymoon there. So Scarborough is rather special, isn't it?' Roger could also have his petulant moods at times.

'Of course it's special, darling. But this year we're going to do something different. We're going to France. And that's that.'

Game, set, and match.

When I heard I was going to France I was absolutely thrilled. Also a little worried, as it would be a lot of hard work and I wasn't exactly in shape. That was putting it mildly. A good run to Scarborough was one thing, a marathon to the middle of France another entirely. Hang it, I didn't even know how far the middle of France was, and as there wasn't a map in the garage there was nothing I could refer to. I would need to talk to Henri the next time I saw him.

I didn't have to wait long as Roger and Lawrence usually arrived home from work at about the same time.

'Henri, how far is it from here to the Dordogne?' I pronounced this Dor-dog-knee as cars don't take French lessons.

'To where, mon ami?'

'The Dor-dog-knee.'

'Ze Dor-dog-knee? Ees it a pub, mon brave?'

'No, no. It's in France. Something to do with Peri-gord.'

'Zut alors! You mean la Dordogne! One of the most beautiful regions in the whole of la France! C'est magnifique! C'est jolie! Quelle rivière! 'Ow I could go on and on about eet!' he enthused, rolling his headlights. 'I would say zat eet's about seven hundred kilometres from here to ze north of la Dordogne.'

Seven hundred kilometres! Wow! That was nearly… wait a minute, let me see… 450 miles! That was over a hundred miles further than Scarborough! This really was going to be a test.

'I've never been driven that far Henri. What's the journey like?'

'Eet depends on ze traffeeq. Eet's very different in la France of course. Ze roads are zat much quieter and sometimes zey can really shake you up! But ze trick is to take your time – mon dieu, why 'urry? Zere's all ze time in ze world wizzout 'aving to speed! You Eengleesh… rush, rush, rush everywhere! And what pleasure to drive on ze right side of ze road. Aah, sheer joy!'

'What do you mean the right side of the road? The left is the right side of the road, isn't it?'

'Oh, non, non, non. Ze right is ze right side. Ze left is ze wrong side. Zey all know zat over zere.'

'Do you mean to say drivers use the right side of the road? How can they see to overtake?'

'Ah, mon ami, you are so naïve! Ze cars are made different over zere. Zey have ze steering wheel on ze left. I am different to many of my countrymen wiz my steering wheel on ze right, because I was destined to live my life 'ere.'

'But I've never been on the right. I wouldn't know what to do! And my lights – they'd point in the wrong direction. I couldn't see where I was going!'

'Don't panic, Roger would provide you wiz a special pair of glasses so you would 'ave no problems with seeing. Of course, if 'e 'asn't driven on ze right before, zere is a much greater chance of… well… 'aving an accident.'

What had been a little apprehension now turned to full-blown anxiety. Roger had only undertaken the regulation drive to Scarborough, never needing to concern himself with anything but where to stop for the picnic they held en route to the Little Beach, their customary holiday hotel.

'Is there anything else I should know?'

'Maybe a few zings…'

'Such as?'

'OK. Don't expect anyone to let you in from a side road – mon Dieu, impensable! Don't upset ze tractors as zey will crush you if you do, comme un petit souris! Don't give way to ze roundabout, or you will be punished, incroyable! And ze traffic lights… zey can be… well, a leetle unpredictable. And ze signs… how zey love to play hide and seek! And don't let Roger wash you. Eet's seen as bad taste. Ze French only wash when we need to – and never on public 'olidays!' He shrugged his wings in the manner unique to those of a Gallic origin.

He was enjoying this. With every exclamation I was feeling more and more twitchy, uncertain as to whether my romantic imagination had run away with me, instead of considering the reality of a stressed Roger conducting an accident-free journey through previously unknown perils which, according to Henri, were lying in wait for the unaware in his native country.

' 'Owever, mon ami, you should not be concerned. Zere are many, many old ones like you en France. Over zere you will be treated wiz more than a leetle respect and courtesy. Probably.'

That was novel. There was scant respect for someone of my vintage on the roads in Britain.

'Come on, Henri, be serious! It can't be as dangerous as you make out. Can it?'

'Maybe I do exaggerate un petit peu…' he answered, with a twinkle in his headlights.

The day of our departure soon arrived. It was glorious, with the early morning rays of sunshine streaming through the garage's sparkling windows. I had been deep in conversation with the garage the evening before and he'd counselled that the journey should be an experience never to be forgotten. It must be approached with a positive attitude no matter what unknowns lay ahead. Then the garage would have some great tales to embellish.

Thoughts of the coming adventure had been running through my mind for several weeks now, as we drove through the hustle and bustle of rush hour traffic to and from Roger's place of work. I reassured myself with the knowledge that Roger wasn't a bad driver – he and I had never been involved in any accidents, which was quite surprising given the harum-scarum younger generation of drivers taking to the roads. This was all the more remarkable as the population of cars seemed to have exploded since the turn of the decade and the roads were more crowded than ever.

Yes, I was sure we'd be OK.

'Bon vacances,' whispered Henri, as Roger turned off the drive. 'A bientôt, mon ami, and mind zose crazy French drivers!'

The journey to Portsmouth was pure hell. We crawled through Tiverton, Taunton, Salisbury and Southampton before finally arriving at the ferry terminal. I could feel the tension in Roger as he tightly gripped my steering wheel, rhythmically depressing and releasing my clutch and brake pedals. I never knew there were so many bottlenecks on the West Country roads, or so many places where there was a likelihood of getting stuck behind a slow-moving lorry or tractor. By the end of the journey my joints were aching. After a six-hour slog, all of us, Sylvia included, were completely worn out.

'My God, thank heavens that's over,' puffed Roger as we joined the snaking lines waiting to board the next ferry. 'I hope France isn't like this.'

'From what I've heard, darling, there's hardly any traffic where we're going. France is rather in the middle ages as far as traffic is concerned, and it's such a big place there's plenty of room for all.'

I was mightily relieved to hear it.

They left me with a deck full of equally tired cars and went topsides to join the rest of the passengers. I must have fallen asleep down in the cavernous bowels of the cross-channel ferry. No doubt the gentle rolling of the ship combined with the low rumble from the distant engines had rocked me to sleep like a baby in a crib.

Next thing I knew I was stung into life by the turn of my ignition key. Light flooded into the ferry as its great jaws opened, and all around drivers were starting the engines of their cars. Four hours had passed in a flash.

Bonjour la France.

On disembarking we drove in single file through the terminal until we reached the connecting road that would take us through Caen. I was now on the 'wrong' side of the road for the first time. At the start it was very scary as my instinct told me I must be breaking some unknown rule as I followed the other Brits out of town in a cautious, winding line. Peugeots, Renaults and Citroens viewed us all with slightly amused looks on their grilles as we traipsed through the port before splitting up en route to our various destinations.

Once out of Caen the traffic dwindled to almost nothing. It was unbelievable. After the crowded roads of the West Country, France was amazingly traffic-free. Being able to relax helped me to gradually become used to life on the 'right' side of the road.

'Bonjour, monsieur,' uttered a battered 2CV as he trundled past.

Two minutes later we passed a Renault 8 in a lay-by. 'Bonjour, monsieur,' she chirruped. 'Il fait beau, non?'

I was taken aback. I could tell how polite they were by their tone, even if I hadn't a clue what they were saying. Courtesy had long disappeared from the frenetic roads of England where nobody would make time for such pleasantries. A change had also come over Roger, who was driving me in a much more laid-back way than he did when we were pushed along on the commuter roads to Barchester before we hit the inescapable rush-hour jams.

We stopped at a small roadside cafe after about an hour, parking next to a Rover 800. As Roger and Sylvia departed for their refreshments I turned to the Rover.

'Hello. You here on holiday?' I queried.

'Yes, we come here every year. Fantastic isn't it? This your first time?'

'Yes, it is.'

'You'll love it. Where are you heading?'

'We're off to the Dordogne.'

'Bloody marvellous. We're staying in Bergerac.'

We were the only two cars in the car park. I nodded across at the road. 'Where is everyone?'

'It's always like this, apart from Paris of course. That place is a nightmare. Out in the country… well, as I said, it's always like this.'

'Don't the French have many cars?' I asked.

'Of course they do! But remember that France is much larger than the UK so the place doesn't appear congested. Everything's much more spread out. That's why I like coming here after all the rushing about back home. I can take it easy for a week or two. Some days they don't even take me off the drive.'

'Just like it used to be when I was young,' I sighed.

'I don't think it was quite this quiet, even when you were young,' he contested.

'No, you're probably right. Memory can be selective.'

'Mine are thinking of coming to live here permanently,' he added. 'Good for them but not for me. I know they'll have to sell me, even though I've been with them for five years. It doesn't make sense having a right-hand drive here.'

His driver had been seduced by what later came to be known as 'the English Migration'. It started with the immense popularity of Peter Mayle's *A Year in Provence* published in 1989, which fired the romantic imaginations of a nation tired with dreary weather, mediocre government, and the stress of a crowded Britain. Droves of Britons were to sell up and leave their homeland for the sunnier climates and more laid-back lifestyles of Spain and France, completely oblivious to the cultural changes and challenges they would face there. The outpouring left a vacuum which in later years was to be filled by invading hordes of Eastern Europeans.

The journey through France was magnificent, taken at a leisurely pace that I was unaccustomed to in the West Country.

On that first day we passed through the towns of Falaise and Alencon before arriving at Le Mans, the first of our overnight stops. Le Mans is a revered place for us cars. We hold it in the same awe and respect as Moslems regard Mecca, Catholics the Vatican, and Jews Jerusalem. The 'Le Mans start' has a special meaning for us as it's the only time when we can actually get drivers to run across a road and jump into us to begin a race. Imagine!

We continued south the next day passing through Saint-Cyr-sur-Loire, stopping for lunch at Chauvigny. After lunch we passed through Lussac-les-Châteaux, Bellac, Limoges, Brive-la-Gaillarde, La Feuillade and Saint-Crépin-et-Carlucet, before arriving at our destination, Sarlat la Canada. What a day that was, travelling nearly 250 miles in all.

And you know what? I wasn't in the least bit tired. The journey had been traffic-free, idiot-free, stress-free and carefree. The sun had shone the whole way and the countryside had been absolutely beautiful.

I could get used to this.

Having just been parked I was enjoying the shade afforded by a row of lime trees in a street running off the Place de la Liberté. We had driven in to Sarlat on a Saturday so that Roger and Sylvia could visit the street market, and get a real flavour of rural France. There had been some difficulty finding a space at first, owing to the crowds converging on the town, but thanks to the kindness of a local resident who offered to let Roger park me in his unoccupied space, we were able to be close to the main market. From here I had a spectacular view of the medieval buildings around which the market was situated. The lively and friendly banter of the stallholders, and the smells and tastes of the food, drifted lazily in the air.

The cloudless sky was the colour of cornflower and there was stillness in the air. This would be a good time to have forty winks.

Then she passed me, just as I was nodding off.

Topless.

A stunningly attractive Alfa Romeo Spider.

My headlights felt as though they were on stalks as she passed languidly by. I just couldn't stop looking at her. Bright red, blemish-free, with the shiniest chrome work you could imagine.

And her wheels! Mama mia! She was even more exquisite than the Spitfire that used to live in our road.

Then she made a right turn and was gone. Had I been dreaming?

In the main agent's I had seen pictures of a Spider pinned up on the walls in the service area. The mechanics drooled over the sleek lines, and droned on about the sporting performance for which Alfa is famous. From the first time I saw those pictures I had dreamt of meeting a Spider, but they were a very uncommon sight on the roads of Britain and I had yet to see one in the flesh.

Until now. The photos didn't do her justice.

And all I had enjoyed was a fleeting glimpse of her beauty.

Three days later I saw the Spider again. We were driving along the Avenue Gambetta on our way to Montignac and I glimpsed her turning into Boulevard Nessmann. On this occasion Sylvia had directed Roger to call into town on the way to stock up with a bottle of suntan lotion for the day's outing.

Parking in the Rue Gaubert, they locked me up and disappeared to do the necessary shopping. The street was quiet at this time of the morning and I was the only car around.

Then the Spider appeared around the corner, slowed down, and stopped almost directly opposite me. Her driver was a short, swarthy man, immaculately dressed in a cream suit which covered a bright blue, open-neck shirt. He got out of the Spider, locked her door and strolled down the street toward the shops.

There was a long silence. Should I attempt to start a conversation? What would I say? Would she understand me? (Cars only understand the language of the country where they're made. I knew she'd been made in Italy so assumed she would only understand Italian.)

'You have travelled far?' The question jumped on me from across the street. Delivered in impeccable English. Looking up, I could see the Alfa gazing straight at me.

'You speak English?' I asked. What a stupid question!

'Of course.'

It was the way she said it that put me on the back foot. The way foreigners unknowingly use 'of course' as if you're an imbecile. Not their fault, it's just another subtle pitfall of the English language.

'My driver, the Conte del'Ortissimo is married to an English lady. They speak English all the time. Where in England do you live?'

'Near to Barchester. Do you know it?'

'No, I'm afraid I do not. I have friends in England who live in Surrey, I think it's called.'

'Surrey. That's quite a distance from me.' Memories wriggled themselves out of the recesses of my mind and burst into the clear light of recollection. 'I had some acquaintances in Surrey, and they were Italian. But that was a long time ago.' I was reminded of those happy occasions spent with Bertie and his Italian friends before the Buntings inexplicably stopped visiting Conrad Quinney.

'You did? What were their names?'

'Let me see. There was Maserati Merak, Dino Ferrari and...'

'No!' she cut in. 'It is not possible!'

'I beg your pardon?' I was taken aback by her outburst.

'This Dino... was he red?' she enquired.

'Yes, Rosso I think he described himself as.'

'And did he belong to a certain Mr Moss?'

'I believe he did.'

There was a sharp intake of breath, followed by a long pause.

'It is my Dino. Oh, my God.'

What an unbelievable coincidence. Two strangers brought together on holiday in rural France, sharing the same acquaintance from our past. Well, I say acquaintance. In her case it was more than that, as I was soon to discover. While our drivers were away she told me the tale of the relationship she'd had with Dino Ferrari more than ten years previously.

The Conte had been quite a collector of sports cars before an ugly divorce from his first wife separated him from much of his inherited wealth. His family estate, close to the Tuscan town of Lucca, often reverberated with the roar of a high-powered engine as the Conte took one of his supercars out for a spin. The Contessa's tastes were much less raw, and she liked the comfort of her little red sports car. An Alfa Spider. The very same Alfa Spider that was talking to me now.

'We went everywhere together, the Contessa and I. She was a

very good driver. Very fast, but very confident. And so beautiful. But alas, she and the Conte just couldn't get on. It was rumoured they'd married too young and had simply grown apart. She pursued her interests and he pursued his.'

'Cars?' I ventured.

'Cars and drinking. A very bad mixture. The drinking was to get worse, the arguments more heated and in the end he told her they'd have to part. She agreed. Their divorce should have been a straightforward affair. Unfortunately for the Conte, her father was a notorious advocate who nursed an oversized ego. Coming from a poor family he relished the thought of having a tilt at the aristocracy even though his daughter had married into the ruling classes. The Conte gave him the perfect opportunity and he grabbed it. Of course, the Conte's lawyer was not going to be bested. From the day the lawyers got involved the Conte and Contessa were caught up in a blizzard of claim and counterclaim from which there was no shelter. It turned into a totally unnecessary and bitter court case in the end. Sorry, I am getting ahead of myself. It is about Dino we are talking.'

'Please, go on.'

'Yes, Dino. I remember the first day the Conte brought him to the castello. We could hear the whine of his mighty engine all the way from across the valley as the Conte guided him round the winding road to his new home. There were other Ferraris at the castello, but Dino's reputation preceded him. It was said that he was the most handsome Ferrari ever produced. When he finally sprinted down the long, straight drive that led to the massive oak doors of the ancestral home we all stared in disbelief. He was stunningly good-looking.'

'That sounds like Dino,' I mused.

'Our headlights met within moments of his parking. I felt something magical inside. He looked at me and with his rich, rumbling voice, introduced himself and asked me about my driver. He was so charming, a complete gentleman. Looking back on it, I am now sure it was love at first sight. For both of us.'

(I'd heard of this strange thing, 'love', which wreaked havoc with the drivers from time to time. But until now I hadn't met any car that had suffered from the affliction.)

'We spent many days after that, talking and talking. Dino had so many interesting stories! And could he make me laugh! He was always happy, even on the cloudiest of days. Nothing got him down.' She sighed. 'But he arrived too late. The Conte and Contessa were in the throes of divorce proceedings and the gods were smiling on her father. He won the case and the Contessa got to keep the castello and a large part of the Conte's fortune. He was forced to live in a large house owned by the estate in Lucca and sell all his cars. Except me. He chose to keep me as a final dig at the Contessa and her father. I remember Dino being collected one day shortly before the Conte moved to Lucca. By an Englishman. The man's name was Mr Moss. Dino and I never even got to say goodbye properly to each other. I was heartbroken. I never heard from him again after that.'

She wouldn't have done, of course. Cars can't write to each other.

Football Match (1993)

Wouldn't you feel silly with a bright yellow-and-black-striped scarf trailing from your side window as you were being driven along the road?

'What a load of bollocks!' chorused a gesticulating passenger at Roger as a bright green Sierra whistled past us in the outside lane, with a red-and-white scarf trailing from each of its rear windows.

'Wanker!' Neville hurled back, leaning across Roger and sticking two fingers in the air at the Sierra's occupants.

'Load of crap! Load of crap!' shouted another passenger as a blue Escort shot past in hot pursuit of the Sierra.

'Is this behaviour normal?' Roger asked Neville with a puzzled frown on his forehead.

'Quite normal, Roger. It's all about passion, see? Brings out the warrior instinct in the male. Haven't you been to a footie match before?'

'Er, no actually, I haven't. I'm more of a rugby man myself.'

Yes, I know. It does seem unbelievable that a man of Roger's age should never have been to a football match. Never stood on the terraces among a crowd of half-crazed fanatics shouting abuse at the opposition supporters and jeering at every mistake the opposing team's players make on the pitch – with everybody from both sides taking it out on the ref.

And for that reason this was the first time I had ever been to a football match myself.

It was a very rare occasion. Roger and Sylvia are creatures of habit. Their routine never varies, week in, week out. Saturday's routine is cast in stone. The morning is 'Roger's time', and this is spent in various ways dependent upon the weather.

Sunny day: Wash me, check my oil, water, tyres, and fill up windscreen washer bottle. Mow lawn. Water plants.

Wet day: Check my oil, water, tyres, fill up windscreen washer bottle. Potter in garage doing sundry jobs. Read newspaper to fill in time before shopping.

Cold winter day: Check my oil, water, tyres, fill up windscreen washer bottle. Potter in garage doing sundry jobs. Tidy garage. Read newspaper to fill in time before shopping.

Saturday afternoon is the weekly shopping trip to Grevington.

So, you see – creatures of habit.

On this particular Saturday an unprecedented change in routine had come about as a result of the coincidence of a number of factors. Sylvia was absent. During the previous week she'd received a call to say that her Aunt Mavis, who'd retired two years ago to the south coast once all three of her nieces were off her hands, had suffered a mild heart attack and was in hospital. Would Sylvia be in a position to spend a week in the vicinity so she could visit Aunt Mavis in hospital in her moment of need? Sylvia agreed immediately. She arranged at short notice to take the week off work, and Roger had dropped her at the railway station the previous Monday morning. He'd argued that he should also take a week's holiday to be with her, but Sylvia would have none of it. Apart from the fact that it would cost them double the amount (Sylvia is very careful with money, always has been ever since she was a little girl) she knew Roger would have nothing to do all day but mope around while she was with the aunt.

The second was Neville, Roger's next-door neighbour. Neville was a regional sales manager with an international software company. Neville could be very persuasive, some might say pushy. I don't think it's that Neville particularly liked Roger; it's just that he didn't appear to have too many friends. In fact, I can't remember many occasions when he and Tracey (his wife) had visitors to their home.

By a stroke of luck, Neville had won a couple of tickets for the local derby match for being the top regional sales manager in his company on account of the sales figures his team had turned in during the previous quarter. He was delighted of course, but was then faced with the dilemma of who to take with him to the match. Tracey hated football and absolutely refused point blank. Lawrence, our other next door neighbour, may have been a possibility, but Neville discounted this immediately as he knew Lawrence was an avid supporter of another, non-local club in the same division.

After considering all the alternatives (even considering not going to the match at all, which would have been too embarrassing in front of his colleagues), he finally decided to approach Roger. Under normal circumstances this would never have happened. Neville thought Roger stuffy and boring, and considered Sylvia aloof and snobbish. Taking advantage of Sylvia's absence, he railroaded Roger.

Roger of course was unhappy about being divorced from his routine, and at first tried to resist the offer, grasping for valid reasons as to why he couldn't go. But they were all very flimsy and, as I said, Neville could be very persuasive.

Reluctantly Roger agreed, and it was arranged that late Saturday morning we would pick Neville up, bedeck me with the scarf, and tootle off to the match. Neville said he didn't want to go in his Jag as it was 'too expensive and might get vandalised'.

Thank you, Neville.

But I was excited. On Sundays I often heard the others cars in the neighbourhood talking about the matches they'd taken drivers to the previous day. Even the cars were infected by the passion of drivers for football.

'Turn left here, mate,' directed Neville.

As we turned off the road I could see in the near distance a huge concrete beast rising from the rows of houses packed around it. It was very impressive.

'That's the Park,' indicated Neville, with pride. 'We'll have to queue for some time, but don't worry; we'll get there in plenty of time for the kick-off.'

'Is it always this busy?' asked Roger.

'Yep. It's not easy trying to get fifteen thousand people in cars down these roads. They were built mostly for foot traffic. They had to tear down five streets just to make way for the car parks.'

'Gosh.'

'Mind if I have a smoke while we're waiting?'

'Well, I…'

'Thanks. I'm gasping for one.' Fishing in his inside pocket, Neville produced an eight-inch-long cigar, took out his lighter, lit up in a billow of smoke and flames, took a deep draught and slowly and contentedly expelled a huge cloud of smoke into my insides.

I could imagine the look of horror that was on Roger's face. Sylvia had a bloodhound's nose and could detect traces of almost any substance, it seemed, with unerring accuracy. She had a pathological dislike of certain smells (stale beer, sprouts, tobacco) and he knew there would be hell to pay if she sensed that someone had been smoking in the car.

Roger was none too keen either.

'Great cigars, these. Got them in Cuba during last year's Golden Achiever trip. Dirt cheap, too. Would you believe twenty for a tenner? They're three quid *each* here! Just shows you what tricks the Chancellor's up to, eh?'

'Shocking. Would you mind if—'

'And the booze! Cuban rum – talk about firewater! Sneaked three bottles through customs. Two fingers to the Chancellor there, eh?'

'We don't like to have—'

'And the women. Wow, the women! Have you ever seen the Salsa, Roger?' Neville made a sensuous wiggling motion with his hands, and took another deep draft and slowly exhaled more smoke to join the grey cloud circling my insides.

'I think we should ope…'

'Pure eroticism the way they move! If only I was single again. Know what I mean? Nudge, nudge, wink, wink.' A third, deep draft and another swirling cloud combined with the other two. By this time Roger could barely see the man sitting just inches away from him.

'Look old chap, would you mind opening the window?' pleaded Roger.

'Sorry. You don't smoke do you?'

'No.'

'Pardon me… I thought everybody does. Where's the button? I can't see for all this smoke.'

It took an age for Roger to get me to a parking space. I never realised (I wouldn't, would I?) that a Cuban cigar takes so long to smoke. It took so long, in fact, that Neville was only three-quarters of the way through the beast when he had to stub it out, an action which must have taken a good two minutes. By which time my insides were stinking of the clinging smoke, most of which had been puffed out of the window only for the breeze to push it straight back in.

'My, that was good. I'll bring a couple over sometime. You really must try one, Roger, it's one of life's great experiences and I know Sylvia will love the aroma. Get her all excited – know what I mean?'

Roger knew what Neville meant, and also knew the effect it would have on Sylvia would definitely not be what Neville anticipated.

'OK, Rog. Let's go. Up the lads!'

'Support the Boro', do you?' asked the maroon Omega parked next to me.

'No. This is the first time my driver has taken me to a football match.'

'Get away! Mine brings me every week in season. Rain, shine, it doesn't matter to him. We'll still be here. Can't beat it, you know. It's a marvellous atmosphere.'

'So they tell me. But you can't see much in a car park, can you?'

'Ah, it's not the seeing that's important. It's the *sound* that matters. Can't you hear it?'

I didn't need to try very hard to hear the noise he was listening to. There was a constant booming of 'Ooh!', 'Agh!' and 'Ref!' intermingled with deep choruses of 'There's only one Billy Thompson!', 'Bo-ro, Bo-ro, Bo-ro!' and a competing 'Ci-ty! Ci-ty! Ci-ty!'

'That doesn't tell you what's going on, it's just shouting,' I said, perplexed.

'You just have to use your imagination for the moment,' advised the Omega. 'You'll get the full story in graphic detail on the drive home. Blow by blow.'

'Bloody referee, must be blind as a bat. Their first goal was clearly offside. Fancy overruling his linesman! I can't believe it. 3–0 to that bunch of losers.'

We were in a slow-moving queue of vehicles waiting to exit from the car parks adjacent to the ground. Neville and Roger had returned to me without a sound. Neville's fists were clenched in anger and his mood was dark. The visiting team, at the bottom of the table as I later learnt during the drive, had had a purple patch in which they had absolutely taken the home side to the cleaners. Like any committed football supporter Neville had taken this personally and was now sitting quietly in the car making the occasional frustrated outburst.

'I swear to God, Rog, that was never in a million years offside. Mullins would have blasted the ball into the back of their net. Bloody referee! Bloody useless cretin!'

'How do you know?' asked Roger innocently.

'How do I know what?' retorted Neville.

'Offside, how do you know it was offside? I'd be interested to know.'

'Christ, Roger, do you doubt my knowledge of the game?'

'No, not at all. But you sound so convinced. I'm curious to know what makes you so sure, that's all.'

'Ah, well, it's a very grey area this one. You'll need to give me your full attention if you want to grasp the intricacies of the offside rule.' Neville dug his hand into his jacket pocket and produced a dog-eared copy of the *Laws of Association Football* and began to flip through the pages until he found Law 11 – Offside.

'Let me see. Ah, here we are, Law 11' He began to cite from the sacred document. 'It is not an offence in itself to be in an offside position. A player shall only be penalised for being in an offside position if, at the moment the ball touches, or is played by one of his team, he is, in the opinion of the referee, involved in active play by: Interfering with play, or interfering with an opponent, or gaining an advantage by being in that position. Gaining an advantage by being in that position means playing a ball that rebounds to him off a goalpost or the crossbar having been in an offside position or playing the ball that rebounds to him off an opponent having been in an offside position.'

'I don't understand,' commented Roger, a deep furrow creasing his brow.

'Well it's… a grey area, as I said.'

'Would you explain it to me, as I haven't a clue what it means?'

'OK. We'll do it bit by bit. Let me see. The offside position. Did you get that bit?

'No.'

'Right. A player is in an offside position if, at the moment the ball touches, or is played by one of his team, he is involved in active play by: Interfering with play, or interfering with an opponent, or gaining an advantage by being in that position. Gaining an advantage by being in that position means playing a ball that rebounds to him off a goalpost or the crossbar having been in an offside position or playing the ball that rebounds to him off an opponent having been in an offside position.'

'Right,' noted Roger hesitatingly, pursing his lips. 'But you missed the bit out about in the opinion of the referee.'

'That's why I said it's a grey area,' stressed Neville.

'But it's not is it?' countered Roger. 'It's not grey if the referee is the sole arbiter and has the final say.'

'Look Roger, I know you're well-meaning, but frankly you know bugger all about footie. That partially sighted ref clearly made the wrong decision giving Mullins offside. For God's sake the ref was ten yards away! He couldn't possibly have made the right call.'

'I still don't understand, really. If the referee's decision is final—'

'Stick to rugby,' grumbled Neville, producing another cigar.

Neighbours (1995)

'Turned out nice again, Rog,' remarked Neville, leaning on his shiny, black Jaguar XJ6, smoking a Cuban.

'They say it's going to remain like that all weekend, Neville,' commented Roger, thankful that he was upwind.

'Was it the BBC or ITV said that?'

'BBC I think.'

'Only last night I'm sure the weather chap on ITV said that it would be sunny early on, turning overcast later with the possibility of rain. If so, what's the point in cleaning your car now if it's going to rain later? There's so much muck in the atmosphere nowadays I can guarantee it'll end up covered in dirt as soon as it rains.'

'*The Times* said there would be light drizzle at the start of the day, improving to bright sunshine later. Top temperature of eighty-six degrees Fahrenheit.' Roger was an avid reader of *The Times* and attempted the crossword every day while on his lunch break.

'Is that so? According to *The Sun*, it should be overcast this morning turning to rain later.' Neville was rather more Bohemian in his tastes and was a keen follower of the tits of the Page Three girls. 'It's no use if you're thinking of polishing the motor is it? Could be halfway through when it buckets down. I'll just run the Jag down to the valeting boys in Tottiecombe. Much less hassle.'

'I read in the *Telegraph* that we're going to have a heatwave starting today,' chipped in Lawrence, our other next-door neighbour.

'Hi, Lol, how's tricks?' shouted Neville, waving the cigar.

Lawrence grimaced and carried on with washing the down-stairs windows.

And so it went on. Everyone and no one knew what the weather was going to do. No matter how many sources they consulted it was inevitable that no consensus would be reached.

But the weather is extremely important to drivers of course. Without knowledge of the weather how could they possibly arrange the weekend's activities with their families and friends?

'If it looks fine we thought we might go to Wookey Hole tomorrow for the day,' said Roger.

'Wouldn't want to be there if it rains, a bit too dangerous if the ground's wet,' opined Lawrence. 'We went last year with the kids and the mother-in-law. Lovely weather when we set out, but by the time we were halfway down the Hole, the heavens opened. It got really wet underfoot, I tell you. We nearly lost the mother-in-law when she slipped and almost slid into the underground river. Mind you, that would have been worthwhile in itself. Sorry, I prevented her from falling!' Chuckles all round.

'Do you think you'll still go, given the forecast?'

'Which forecast?'

'BBC one, I think.'

At this point all three halted their activities (or inactivity in Neville's case) to collectively engage in a conversation with the postman, just as I was enjoying having my boot scrubbed with warm, soapy water and a lovely new, yellow sponge. The Jaguar had that smug, contented look of one about to be pampered by a professional. As always, Lawrence's BMW 520 squatted sour-faced on his drive.

'I say, chaps, is the weather all they ever think about?' whispered the Jag. 'You'd think there was something more… interesting.'

'Ja, und lest veek mine spent zree hours dezeydink vezer or no to drife me to verk or take zer train. Vot stupid behaviour! He nose fery vell how I enjoy ze rain viz my owtoematic vipers! Vhy in Got's name did I hef to end up in ziz place ven I could be in zer Schwarzwald!'

I wondered if all Germans were as acerbic as this one.

The foreign makes had truly taken over. It was now 1995 and much had changed since the largest maker went to the wall. In my road only myself, the MGF at Number 33, the Rover 600 at Number 2 and the Jaguar XJ of Neville's could claim to be natives. All the rest were foreigners – Peugeots, Renaults, VWs, Audis, Citroëns, BMWs, Alfas, Nissans, Hondas, Toyotas.

What was worse, they were of a different generation from me (actually several generations) and their values, language, and attitude towards their drivers were very different to mine.

As an example, when a youngster I had been taught to respect my elders, and the makers impressed on us all a Code of Conduct by which we were to govern our relationship with those around us. Rule 4 of the Code ran along the following lines:

4(i)   Don't play games with the bikes. They have been around a lot longer than you have and they'll probably be here when you're long gone.

4(ii)   Don't bully the motorbikes. They may be smaller than you but if they gang up there could be serious trouble.

4(iii) Don't take on the lorries. You will never, repeat never, win an argument with a lorry.

4(iv)   Don't always do what the drivers want you to do. Experience has proven they are prone to errors of judgement. The consequences could be fatal.

4(v)   Do give clear warning of your intentions to speed up, slow down, turn left or turn right. The designers have had the good foresight to provide you with lights and indicators specifically for this purpose.

4(vi)   Do defer to the pedestrians. They need to cross the road many times in the course of their everyday lives, and the footpath was invented especially for them. They are special.

4(vii) Do be cautious of animals that have a strange fascination for the road. Foxes, stoats, weasels and badgers that dash across, hedgehogs that walk along, rabbits that stop and stare at you, and particularly pheasants, which have a kamikaze commitment to flying in your face at every opportunity.

4(viii) Do be aware of the sharp bends. The road has a tendency to curl like a coiled snake, and like a snake it has the ability to unwind at breakneck speeds.

4(ix)   Do read the signs that the road has put out for you. If the road has requested you to slow down there is a reason for it. The road is not given to frivolity and you will not find sympathy if the signs are ignored.

Yes, Rule 4 was so sacrosanct it was also translated as part of the driver's *Highway Code* and impressed firmly on learner drivers when they attended driving lessons. The examiners were a bunch to be feared in those days. Without their say learner drivers were consigned to the drive until the *Highway Code* had been fully taken on board and could be regurgitated, almost verbatim. When the examiners gave the learners permission to use the road without supervision, Rule 4 became unknowingly hardwired into their behaviour, and was adhered to and applied with the utmost rigour.

How things change. I blame the foreign makes to some degree. How could they be expected to understand the subtleties and nuances of Rule 4 in a language with which they are not familiar?

Admittedly though, it's not all the foreign makes' fault. There has been a marked change in the drivers' behaviour also. And not just on the road. It probably started in the mid-eighties when social attitudes began to change. It was around the time that politicians started to promote the culture of 'Me First'. Like many politicians' ideas it should have been scrambled before it hatched. The concept was that one shouldn't depend on the activities of others to get what one wanted in life. One should simply go out and grab it for oneself. Unfortunately 'Me First' has been applied a little too literally, resulting in what has now become commonly known as the 'Me First Bugger Everyone Else' approach to living.

A good example of this can be seen on the road. At one time drivers had to scrimp and save in order to afford whatever transport they aspired to – be it one of us, or a motorbike. The corollary was that the number of us on the road was kept to a manageable level. Only in the very largest cities were there occasional queues. In the country lanes we could travel for miles and hardly see each other.

'Me First' changed all that. The banks ruthlessly exploited the culture of 'Me First' to their own advantage. They made it easy for drivers to acquire more and more of us by literally throwing money at them. (One outcome of this was that the main agents were forced to bring in the foreign makes to satisfy demand – there just weren't enough of us locals to go around now that the largest maker had gone belly-up.) And, my, how the drivers bought!

Within a short space of time there were jams everywhere. Not just the big cities, but in the towns and villages over a large part of the country, even in the burgeoning supermarket car parks. Tempers started to fray, and drivers and foreign makes began to ignore and even abuse Rule 4. Worst of all hit were the roads. They just couldn't cope with blocked arteries. It got so bad the politicians had to build whole new bypasses to relieve the congestion – at a huge cost to the taxpayer.

But it was too late. 'Me First' had taken hold and was firmly rooted. Like a malignant cancer it spread to every part of society. Whereas previously drives had to accommodate one, or occasionally two, of us, suddenly there were three and sometimes four as a household trained yet another new learner. And did the learner drivers embrace the 'Me First' culture? They sure did! They thirsted to get out on to the road. Of course, the first thing a learner driver did on passing muster in the eyes of an examiner was to go to the bank and the bank would gladly provide the funds to go and buy a car. What a time the main dealers had! And what a time the dodgy dealers had!

So what happened to Rule 4?

Not surprisingly, after a learner driver was allowed unaccompanied passage on the road, Rule 4 faded into the background to be replaced by the 'Me First' adaptation of Rule 4, which can now be stated in its revised form as:

4(i)   Don't give a shit about the bikes. They're only small and what does it matter if they get knocked about from time to time? Nobody listens to them anyway. They can always use the footpath.

4(ii)   Don't pay any attention to the motorbikes. If they do gang up (which isn't likely) we can always drive straight through them.

4(iii)   Don't worry about the lorries. They're much slower than us now and we can run rings around them. And that can be quite fun.

4(iv)   Do always obey the drivers. They have tremendous power and if they don't like you they'll trade you in. There is no loyalty nowadays.

4(v)   Don't give clear warning of your intentions to speed up, slow down, turn left or turn right. It's up to the other drivers to anticipate your every move. If they can't, tough for them.

4(vi)   Do try to annoy the pedestrians. It can be tremendously amusing to frustrate them as they try to cross the road. This forces them to use the footpath where they will fight with the bikes.

4(vii)   Do try to destroy any animals that have a strange fascination for the road. It's a great game to play. If you're lucky (and accurate) and happen to hit a rabbit or pheasant, the driver will usually stop and quietly slip the (hopefully) dead animal into the boot. They'll make a great meal later. You'll be in his good books for ever.

4(viii)   Do try to beat the sharp bends. That's what they're there for isn't it? You know the designers have made you so that you can negotiate them on two wheels if desired.

4(ix)   Do ignore the signs that the road has put out for you. It's about time the road got a sense of humour.

The chat with the postman about the previous evening's football over, the three neighbours returned to their tasks. Well, Roger and Lawrence did.

'I might suggest we go to Milverton later on. The missus likes to go shopping and it gives me a chance to escape any DIY jobs she's got for me,' called Neville.

'Not that you've ever done any,' muttered Lawrence to himself on resuming his window cleaning.

'That wouldn't work for me, Neville,' added Roger, sneakily looking around to see whether he was being observed, or could be overheard by Sylvia. 'I've got my list and the list must be observed. Unless of course she decides we're going shopping.'

'They're all the same, aren't they? I think it's an obsession. Like gambling or something.'

There was a collective sigh and shaking of heads.

Certain subjects are guaranteed to bond any strangers as long as they are male. Football, sex, the weather – and the dislike of shopping.

As it is said, men are from Mars, and women are from Venus.

Gossip and Rumour (1997)

One bright summer day Roger was washing the dishes (Sylvia didn't believe in dishwashers – 'They always leave disgusting remains on the plates and pans. You're *much* better at it, darling') when she remarked, 'Have you heard about Neville? Sheila told me he was seen with a blonde woman in Tottiecombe last week, and guess what? They were linking – yes, actually linking – arms. What do you think of that?'

Sheila was head librarian of the Comberton library. What she didn't know about the goings-on in the village wasn't worth knowing. She wasn't a gossip, just an incredible fount of knowledge concerning the village's activities. Luckily for Sylvia, she was also the wife of Lawrence, the next-door neighbour. Whatever information Sheila hoovered up from her numerous informants, it wouldn't be too long before it was passed on to Sylvia.

'It wouldn't surprise me. I reckon he's a bit of a lad. It's those shifty eyes of his. And his eyebrows meet in the middle. They say you can never trust anyone whose eyebrows meet in the middle,' commented Roger, describing a line with the tip of his forefinger across the bridge of his nose. 'And he's in sales.'

'Precisely. So next time you're out talking to him you might like to ask – subtly, of course – who the lady was who was seen with him last week?' This was not so much a request from Sylvia as a demand.

Fifteen minutes later Roger moved me from the garage on to the drive, and was just about to start lathering me with some lovely warm water containing Turtle Wax, my favourite, when Neville strode out of his front door and waved to him.

'Turned out nice again, Rog,' called Neville, puffing on a Henri Winterman half-corona. The Jag had recently disappeared to be replaced by a Renault Safrane, a funny-looking car which always seemed to have a leer on his grille. Around here he was getting a reputation, too. A bad reputation.

'Morning, Neville. Beautiful day,' greeted Roger.

'Hi, Lol. Great weather,' shouted Neville across to Lawrence.

'Super,' replied Lawrence, stuck halfway into his Volvo (the sour-faced BMW had been traded in), with the extension hose on his vacuum cleaner in hand.

The usual weather discussion continued until Neville fished in his pocket to retrieve and light another cigar. Whereas Cubans lasted the best part of an hour, the Henri Wintermans were reduced to a stub in a little over twenty minutes. Neville's love of cigars was getting to be a very expensive habit.

'Neville,' Roger whispered conspiratorially, sidling over to the low privet hedge that defined the boundary between their properties. 'Do you mind if I ask you something?'

'No, you can't borrow any money from me, mate,' bantered Neville.

'No, no. Seriously.'

'OK. Shoot.'

'A hypothetical question for you. If you were seen with an attractive lady on your arm in town how would you explain it to your wife if she found out?'

'Ah, tricky one, mate. Who is she?' teased Neville.

'Pardon?' asked Roger, puzzled.

'Who is she? The woman you're having an affair with.'

'I'm not having an affair.'

'Then why is she hanging on to your arm?'

'She's not hanging on my arm. It's hypothetical.'

'Come, come, old son. This is Neville you're speaking to. I've never been known to reveal a secret.' Neville gave Roger a knowing wink as if to bear out that he was the last person with whom you'd want to share your secrets.

Then an invisible voice shrilled from inside the house.

'Roger, Roger! Would you please answer the phone? My hands are full.'

'Coming, darling,' and into the house scooted Roger.

As soon as he was out of sight Neville dashed into his house and blurted to Tracey, his beloved. 'Love, did you know that Roger's having an affair?'

'Never! Who told you that?'

'He did! Just now! And guess what? He's been seen with her in town, in flagrante delicto! What do you think Sylvia will do when she finds out?'

'The snooty bitch'll kill him! My God, who would have thought it? He's hardly a Casanova is he? Mind you, they do say still waters run deep. How long has it been going on?'

'No idea. Maybe for ages. I have noticed he's been acting rather strangely recently. Probably his conscience troubling him.'

'Would you believe it? Wait till I tell Sheila.'

'Hey, Sylv, guess what?' teased Roger after he'd dispensed with the 'wrong number' phone call.

'Did you take your shoes off, Roger?' queried a frowning Sylvia, eyeing a suspicious brown stain on the hall carpet.

'Yes, yes. But guess what?' persisted Roger.

'The car won't start?'

'No, no.'

'You've misplaced your glasses?'

'No, no. Much better than that.'

'I give up. Tell me.'

'You're dead right about Neville. He is having an affair.'

'No! He told you so?' Sylvia was suddenly all ears.

'Not in so many words. I asked him a hypothetical question – if he was seen with an attractive lady on his arm in town how he would explain it to his wife if she found out?'

'What did he say to that?'

'Ah, very interesting. I could see by the look in his eyes that I'd touched a nerve. He immediately made a joke of it and asked me who the lady is, as if it was me that had been seen. Guilty as hell, I'd say.'

'Poor Tracey. What has she done to deserve a beast like that? It's not exactly as if he's good-looking or loaded with money.'

'Would it make a difference if he was?'

'It might.' This was spoken with a slight blush on Sylvia's face, followed quickly by, 'But not to me of course. I'm perfectly content with what I've got.' She pecked him on the cheek as if this was irrefutable proof of her undying love.

'I love you,' squeaked Roger.

'I love you, too. Now, hadn't you better finish the car? I'll have to tell Sheila. She'll know what to do with the information.'

The Safrane had a bad reputation. He was very talented, certainly. He could travel round corners like he was on rails. What a body swerve! I had to admire his skills in that area. And could he sprint! At that time (until the Nissan arrived at number 16) he was arguably the fastest thing on four wheels in the cul-de-sac.

And he knew it. That was the root of his problem.

'Leesen to zem, old man. Zey know nuzzink of ze affairs of ze 'eart.' The Renault shot me a glance as Neville stood, puffing away. 'Whereaz I, I am ze love machine. And I can tell you a zink or two. Why, only last week I was deleeberately teased by a Celica. She knew wat she wanted.'

I wasn't really surprised. Celicas had a reputation for forward behaviour. Drivers called them the 'Hairdresser's Car', as a surprisingly large number of them did seem to be owned by hairdressers. They weren't the first to break Rule 6, but they were probably the worst repeat offenders.

'What did she want?' asked the Volvo, in impeccable English. He could have been from the Home Counties if you heard him speak from behind the closed doors of his garage.

'Alors, mon ami. Wat do you zink she wanted?'

'You tell me. It never happens to me.'

'Zat's because you Swedes are so… 'ow you say? Frigeed. You must ave ze thick oil, I zeenk. Eh bien, as I was zaying. She knew wat she wanted. 'ey, old man, do you know wat she wanted?'

Sex was a recurring theme with the Renault.

'I'm sure you'll tell me.'

'She wanted a nudge on 'er rear bomper, zat's wat she wanted. And you know wat? I was just ze one to give 'er one!'

'I think you've got a vivid imagination,' said the Volvo. 'Her driver may just have hit the brakes a little too hard.'

'Merde! Do not question me when I say zeez zings! I tell you she was begging for me to touch 'er bomper!'

'What about Rule 2? I asked innocently.

'Wat of eet, old man? Eet's a stupid rule. As for me, I don't care for eet.'

Oh dear, times had certainly changed. The 'Me First' attitude had spread from the drivers to the cars and had firmly taken root. Old values were being ignored, common courtesies were disregarded and there was a whole generation of new cars that hadn't even bothered to learn, never mind understand the Code.

'And just yesterday,' the Renault continued, 'a Mazda took her top off in front of me! Zis ees ze effect I 'ave on zem, you see.'

Resigned, the Volvo and I looked at each other.

Big Trouble (2000)

'What's wrong, darling?' asked Sylvia, noticing his long face.

'What makes you think something's wrong?' snapped Roger.

'You always kiss me when you arrive home from work. Tonight you didn't.'

'I must have forgotten.'

'You never forget. You haven't missed once in twenty-five years. Is something the matter?'

'No, nothing at all, I just forgot. It's only a small thing anyway.'

'Not to me, it's isn't. Are you going to tell me what's troubling you?'

'I told you – nothing's the matter!' With that, Roger stormed out of the room.

Something was definitely wrong. She'd first detected a change in his manner about two weeks ago. On the Friday night of that week he'd arrived home looking thoroughly worn out. He asked her to cancel the Italian meal that they were planning to have with their friends in Grevington, complaining of listlessness and a splitting headache. Thinking that it was the start of flu she'd dosed him with aspirin, eased him into a hot path, and then packed him off to bed.

His humour didn't improve the following week. On Monday he left late for work. Although she suggested he should have a day off, he insisted on getting up and carrying on business as usual. The dark mood continued throughout the week. Roger was morose and she found it difficult to hold the simplest conversation with him. His replies were either monosyllabic or terse.

She wasn't going to let it drop. Following him into the lounge she said, 'You've been going around like a bear with a sore head for the past fortnight. What in heaven's name is the matter with you?'

'Nothing, I'm fine.' *The Times* was spread wide open hiding Roger, who was immersed in his favourite chair.

'No you're not. Don't lie to me. Put that paper down and talk to me.'

'It's nothing. Please leave me alone.'

'Not until we get to the bottom of this. I've had enough of your moods recently. You don't know what it's like living with someone who hardly notices you're there.'

The paper remained where it was.

'Did you hear me? I'm tired of this!' she shrieked like a banshee.

The paper was suddenly tossed to the floor, and Roger, holding his head between his hands and trembling, burst into tears. Stunned by this show of emotion, Sylvia's mood swiftly changed from anger to concern. She shot across the floor and knelt down beside Roger, cradling an arm round the stricken man. He continued to hold his head in his hands, shaking it repeatedly from side to side.

'Darling, whatever's the matter?'

There was no answer at first, and then he took a deep draught of air, wiped his eyes and began slowly shaking his head.

'I've been made redundant.'

The world stopped spinning.

'Oh my God.'

The signs had all been there, it was just that he'd chosen to ignore them. For quite some time now smaller, more agile and, most importantly, cheaper firms has been nibbling away at Fleesem, Robsem and Crooks's most profitable clients. There was the staggering loss of the Corrigans account, one of the largest high street retailers in the country. Corrigans decided it was time for a change and to give another firm a shot. Or so they said. Of course, accountants usually make poor salesmen and it had been assumed, falsely as it turned out, that the Corrigans business would be renewed by default. So they accepted Corrigans' reasons without any attempt to get at the real problem. No effort was made to understand the client's issues and challenges. If it had been, the firm would have realised that Corrigans were having tough times themselves and had decided to cut costs on major items, one of which was the Fleesem, Robsem and Crooks audit. It broke Mr Robsem's heart to lose a client the firm had had almost since its inception.

Then bang went The Toy Box, another national high street retailer, followed in quick succession by Make It Up, a South West-based DIY company; FlameRight, a large manufacturer of domestic gas fires and boilers; Merryweathers, an outdoor clothing chain; and most recently WestElec, the region's electricity utility.

It didn't go unnoticed that Corrigans and The Toy Box were Roger's personal clients. Once these disappeared over the accounting horizon, he was left to muddle on with a handful of smaller accounts, and even some of these were thinking of placing their business elsewhere. It was now cheaper, much cheaper, to have basic accounting work done offshore in either India or China.

A crisis was beginning to loom in the old established firm.

One afternoon, as Roger was brewing himself a cup of tea he received an email asking him to attend a meeting in Mr Robsem's office at four o'clock. This was quite unusual as the managing partner was not known for his liking of electronic communications, and much preferred to invite people to meetings by asking them face-to-face.

The email had been sent to Roger, Amrit Hattangady, Kevin Hong, Marsha Gallup, Tadesh Szwyevewski, Marcus Shelby, and David Dell-Bywater. Nothing odd there, thought Roger. They were all junior partners of the firm, had all been promoted at more or less the same time, and had all lost business to the new breed of predatory accounting firms. But for the next two hours his mind wouldn't leave him alone as it kept coming back to the question of why they had been called into Robsem's office.

At precisely ten minutes to four he got up from his desk, walked through the varnished fire door that separated his open-plan office from the stairwell, and ascended the single flight of stairs to the top floor where the two senior partners had their palatial offices and suite of rooms. He wasn't the first to arrive. Dell-Bywater narrowly edged him and was standing next to the water cooler on the landing.

'I say, Rog, know what's this is all about?' asked Dell-Bywater in his marble-smooth voice, the product of a privileged education thanks to Harrow and Durham University.

'Not a clue, David. It's very unusual, isn't it?'

'It certainly is, old man. Wouldn't be surprised if we were in line for a bonus, though. All the wallahs on the mailing list have been partners for some time, and we surely deserve some recognition for our efforts.'

Roger thought about this and reasoned it was a fair guess. He was about to resume the conversation when there was the shuffling of feet on the concrete stairs as Amrit Hattangady, Kevin Hong, Marsha Gallup, Marcus Shelby and Tadesh Szwyevewski appeared from under the landing, en masse. What a mix they were. Amrit Hattangady, a tall, dark-skinned, spindly man with jet-black hair and sloping shoulders. Kevin Hong, about two-thirds his height and half again his width, wearing the thickest-lensed spectacles you could imagine. Marsha Gallup, the power dresser in the office, rumoured to be a lesbian, resplendent in a padded-shoulder, grey-pinstripe suit. Tadesh Szwyevewski, grossly overweight with a nicotine-stained grey moustache and pockmarked face and, lolling along at the back, Marcus Shelby, black as the ace of spades, athletic, assured and smelling of Old Spice – always popular with the ladies.

The door marked 'J M R Robsem – Managing Partner' opened and a bespectacled bald head peeked out at them. Mr Crooks was evidently in residence in his colleague's office.

'Ah, good, good. I see you're all here,' he noted, quickly taking in the waiting party. 'Do come in.'

The entourage filed into the office where a dour Mr Robsem was sitting on the edge of his lavish desk. To his right was Mrs Mainwaring, the firm's HR manager. He peered over the top of his bifocals at the standing people assembled in front of him.

'Please take a seat, we won't detain you for too long,' began Robsem. 'Mr Crooks,' he acknowledged his colleague with an effete wave of the hand, 'and I have invited you up as we have a very important issue to discuss with you. Mrs Mainwaring needs to be here also in accordance with the firm's personnel policies.' Mrs Mainwaring was acknowledged with a tilt of his silver-haired head.

'As you will be aware the firm is going through some tough times at the moment. Arguably, the toughest in the history of this business. We're facing competition from all sorts of newcomers, and many of our clients are adopting cost-cutting measures. As we all know, the annual audit is low hanging fruit for our competitors. We have only to look at Corrigans and The Toy Box to see how easily it can happen,' he added, staring straight at Roger. 'We can see the profile of accounting services changing. It would appear our clients are no longer satisfied with traditional offerings, they are demanding all sorts of business assistance – business strategy, IT consultancy, and so forth, areas where, unfortunately, this firm currently has little or no expertise. As you know, our basic traditional services are also being attacked by the offshore providers. It's not the way it used to be, I'm afraid.'

Thanks to the Old Guard, many in the room were thinking. We should have changed long ago but these two got stuck in their ways. The elder statesmen had treated the changes as 'fads and fashion'. It was only when they received the body blow from Corrigans that they realised the world had turned on its axis, had turned several times to boot. By which time it was too late to react. Time had come for damage limitation.

'After many discussions and taking the advice of our bankers and solicitors, we have come to the conclusion that things need to change, and change quickly. We have sounded out the Tyler Group, which as you know is a reputable firm of management consultants, to advise us and help us to implement the necessary changes in the business. Of course, it will take time, but they have already identified where there needs to be some immediate changes in the firm's structure. As from next week we will be introducing a new Business Advice and Management Division, and an IT Effectiveness Division. There is a great deal that needs to be done and Mrs Mainwaring will be working with Tyler's and us' – he indicated Crooks – 'on the restructuring.'

Glances were exchanged in the audience. So, this was where it was going. There were to be some new appointments of Divisional Heads. Two Divisional Heads. There could be excitement in the old firm!

'Of course, to balance the cost of such an ambitious project, there must be sacrifices.' He paused to let this sink in. 'Mr Crooks and I have taken the decision to downsize certain areas of our traditional business.'

Roger felt his stomach knot. He knew what was coming. Many of the firms' established clients had gone through 'downsizing', 'rightsizing', 'workforce reduction' or 'reduction in force'. Whatever it was termed, people lost their livelihoods. He recalled the recent exchanges between him and Robsem. The loss of Corrigans had been taken badly by the partner, and Roger couldn't help but feel the man blamed him personally.

'First, the matter of the new Divisions. You have probably guessed that we intend to appoint internally as we always have, in recognition of our employees' loyalty and dedication to the firm. You would be right, this is indeed our intent. You have all been invited to this meeting as you are the people who came to mind when we first considered who would be suitable to lead the nascent businesses. We considered your experience, knowledge, contacts, leadership qualities and, dare I say it, salesmanship.' The last word was spoken with a slight curling of the lip, as if Robsem had trodden in something unpleasant. 'Naturally, you all have strengths and weaknesses, so it was a very difficult decision. Very difficult indeed.' Crooks joined him in nodding, and it was like watching a pair of toy dogs that people kept on the rear shelves of their cars. 'Fortunately, we were able to agree and come to a decision. You're all here so we can announce it to you. I trust you will be discreet and wait for the formal announcement to be made?'

A harmonious 'yes' from the floor.

'We'll press on then. First, the Business Advice and Management Division. Mr Crooks?'

Attention switched to the other partner, sitting behind Robsem's mahogany desk and leaning back in his swivel chair. 'Thank you, Mr Robsem. After very careful consideration we have decided to appoint... Marsha... as the new Divisional Head. As you know from her handling of the very tricky CruiseLine account where she actually increased business, and the new Hancock & Fleming business she won – in the face of very stiff competition – Marsha will be an invaluable asset for the fledgling division. Please follow me in congratulating her.' Putting his hands together he began to clap and was joined by the rest of the room, excepting Marsha who was grinning like a Cheshire cat.

'The IT Effectiveness Division, Mr Robsem?'

All eyes swivelled back.

'Thank you, Mr Crooks. Another very difficult decision. So many good candidates. Difficult, difficult, difficult.'

Bums began to squirm on seats. Except for Marsha Gallup's. Hers had taken root.

'Let's not keep them in suspense, eh, Mr Crooks?' teased Robsem, winking at his cohort. 'I'm proud to announce that... Marcus Shelby will lead the IT Effectiveness Division. We all know Marcus is an outstanding accountant. In addition he is probably the most IT-literate person in the business and has deep knowledge of the film industry and excellent relations with the media.'

Everyone in the room knew why. Everyone except Robsem and Crooks. Shelby was beaming and giving a thumbs-up sign.

'Congratulations, Marcus!' piped Crooks. Once again the clapping was renewed.

'Dear me, that's enough excitement for one day,' puffed Robsem, wiping this sweating brow with a sparkling white handkerchief. 'Thank you all for attending. Roger, David... would you kindly stay behind please?'

As the departing group filed out of the door one by one, chattering among themselves, Crooks, Robsem and Mrs Mainwaring formed a huddle and whispered to each other. Tadesh Szwyevewski, the last to leave, closed the door quietly behind him.

'Please sit down, chaps,' invited Robsem, who remained standing and began to pace up and down the room like a caged lion. 'This isn't going to be easy I'm afraid. I mentioned that Mr Crooks and I have taken the decision to downsize certain areas of our traditional business. It was a very hard decision I can tell you, one that we hope we won't ever need to take again. In every war there will always be casualties.'

Robsem's last sentence wasn't well chosen and Roger felt his sphincter twitch. Dell-Bywater was fiddling madly with his tie pin. They didn't dare to look at each other.

'Our decision was based on the underperformance of your groups. We aren't blaming you personally of course, although we do feel – don't we Mr Crooks – that the damaging losses of Corrigans, The Toy Box, FlameRight, Merryweathers, and WestElec could have been... anticipated.' The evil eye fell on Roger and moved to his co-accused.

That was below the belt, thought Roger, and I bet Dell-Bywater's thinking the same.

'There's no easy way to say this, I'm afraid. We've decided to let you go.' There was a collective sigh from Robsem and Crooks while Mrs Mainwaring looked sympathetically at the two unfortunates.

Let us go, go where? Roger couldn't think straight. He glanced at Dell-Bywater, whose jaw had dropped almost to his midriff – Dell-Bywater, once the golden boy of the firm, thought by many to be a fair bet to succeed one or other of the old men who now stood in judgement before them.

'Of course, we'll give you six months' notice in recognition of your many years of service. Naturally, if you prefer to leave immediately we shan't prevent you. You'll be fully compensated financially. Mr Crooks and I would prefer it if you did stay for the duration, of course. We owe that much to you. Do you have any questions?'

Silence. Dell-Bywater had petrified.

'No? In that case I'll ask Mrs Mainwaring to arrange further meetings with you to go through the details. Thank you for coming.' He waved a hand towards the door, which was opened by Mrs Mainwaring.

As if joined at the hip, Roger and Dell-Bywater rose from their chairs and departed through the door, which was closed firmly after them. Halting momentarily, Roger could hear a conversation going on in the room behind him and turned to address Dell-Bywater, but the latter was already halfway down the flight of stairs, cradling his head in his hands.

Roger never fathomed why, at that precise moment, he felt the urge to return to the door. Attuned to the voices he retraced his steps and placed his ear carefully against the thickness of Robsem's door.

'Thank God that's over,' he heard Robsem say.

'You did very well, James. Most convincing. You almost had me fooled with your performance.'

'Thank you, Maurice. Pity we couldn't pick the best ones for the job. Bunting and Dell-Bywater would have been perfect choices.'

Mrs Mainwaring's mellifluous voice cut in the conversation.

'I agree entirely, Mr Robsem. However, you had no choice but to take into account the Race Relations, and Equal Opportunities Acts. If you'd appointed Bunting and Dell-Bywater instead of Gallup and Shelby, or sacked Hattangady, Hong or Szwyevewski you could have laid the firm open to all sorts of accusations. Perhaps even legal actions.'

Roger fainted.

'When did this happen?' asked Sylvia, patting the back of his hand.

'Two weeks ago.'

'And you didn't tell me?'

'I couldn't. I just couldn't bring myself to tell you. After the initial shock wore off it felt… well, it felt that I was somehow letting us down. Letting you down.'

'Well you're not. I knew there were going to be some changes of course, everyone in the office did. The talk's all about the new divisions, though. Nobody's mentioned anything about job losses. We all know the business is struggling in certain areas, but nobody has said it's bad enough to make anyone redundant.'

'Unfortunately it is, and I don't think Dell-Bywater and I will be the only casualties.'

Sylvia gasped in amazement. 'Dell-Bywater? They're making him redundant?'

'Yes.'

'Good God. I thought he was next in line to the throne.'

'I think he did, too. Oh, Sylv, what am I going to do? I'm fifty-seven years old. There's plenty of accountants around much younger, much cheaper, and just as good as I am if I'm honest. Fleesem's doesn't exactly have a reputation as being at the cutting edge so none of the other firms are remotely interested in poaching our staff. What the other firms want now is an accountant who can also sell, and I just can't do that. The thought of it makes my stomach churn.'

'Don't worry, darling. It's not the end of the world. We'll have a good talk about it when you feel the time is right. When have they asked you to leave?'

Roger sighed deeply. It felt as if a concrete block had been lifted off his chest, allowing him to breathe normally once again. The redundancy had been a terrible blow. Just like his father, he wasn't very good at showing his emotions, and had suppressed his reaction to the dreadful news. Should he tell Sylvia? He'd tortured himself with that question. In the end he ended up doing what he usually did – sitting on the fence. He simply avoided conversing with her. Two weeks had passed as quickly as two days.

'They've been very good. I've been given six months.'

'That's very generous – they didn't have to do that. Was it the same for Dell-Bywater?' she asked.

'Yes, but he tells me he'll be taking the money after a month, so I suppose Mr Crooks will announce his leaving 'to pursue other business interests' or some other polite euphemism soon. David will be fine. His wife's wealthy and we all know he doesn't really need to work. He does it because he's bright and it gives him an income of his own. He'll soon fill the time with golf and whatever else he takes up to pass the time. I wouldn't be surprised if he goes into local politics.'

'Oh, well. What's done is done. I don't think we should worry. After all, we're not exactly short of money.'

That's a relief, he thought. Roger's mother had passed away in 1986, surviving his father by eight years. In her will she had left their terraced house and several thousand pounds to her only son. This had helped finance the move to Hazlemere eighteen months later. There had been no need to increase their small mortgage which they now knew must be minuscule in comparison to some of their newer neighbours. Their coffers had been further swelled with the substantial third of Aunt Mavis's estate when she died six years ago.

'No, I suppose not. But what am I going to do?'

'We'll think of something, darling. We'll think of something.

There's plenty of time. Meanwhile just carry on at work as if nothing's going to change.'

But it would. More than they could imagine.

Garden Centre (2002)

It was now nearly twelve months since Roger had departed the familiar world of Robsem, Fleesem and Crooks. Twelve months during which he'd racked his brain to come up with an idea, any idea, as to how he was going to make a living. This must be what writer's block is like, he thought. At first he agreed with Sylvia that he must continue with the same pattern to his days that he had known all his working life. Up at seven o'clock. Wash, shave and get dressed. Breakfast at seven twenty. Ease me out of the garage at seven fifty. Drive to their office (only it wasn't their office any more – it was just Sylvia's) as he now had time to give her a lift there every morning after she had seen to Henry. Drive home and start his 'working' day.

The 'working day' consisted of combing any and every source for an accountancy job vacancy. Conferencing with his personal consultants at two recruitment agencies on a Monday. Poring over the job adverts in the *Barchester Herald* on a Tuesday morning. Writing job applications on Tuesday afternoon. Popping into the Jobcentre on a Wednesday morning. What a waste of time that was. He could easily have got a menial job for £5.20 an hour, but washing dishes at the Barchester Holiday Inn didn't compare with a lifetime of people praising him for his intricate knowledge of the tax system. Scanning the *Daily Telegraph* job pages on a Thursday morning. Writing yet more applications in the afternoon. Friday was a day spent planning job-hunting for the following week. (Roger, a professed technophobe, never realised he could have made life a lot easier for himself by joining the ever-swelling ranks using the World Wide Web.)

When he wasn't job-hunting he was thinking, and the more he thought the less his imagination worked. To Roger, accountancy was his life. It seemed as if the Fates were against him, almost screaming: 'This is the deal, Bunting. We want you to be an accountant. If you can't be an accountant then we're bloody well not going to help you to be anything else!'

Gradually the nature of his 'working day' changed. He began to spend more of his time doing jobs around the house. It started in a small way. Dusting the furniture, vacuuming the carpet, popping down to the village Spar for a bottle of milk. Then more time-consuming tasks took their places on the roster. Mowing the lawn; taking household rubbish to the tip at Milverton; washing and polishing me. In the sixth month of his redundancy he graduated to redecorating the lounge, and built a wooden decking platform in the garden. Tasks of such complexity for the old Roger that he would willingly have shelled out rather than contemplated doing them himself.

His latest and by far most-ambitious project, scheduled for month fifteen and not yet mooted to Sylvia, was the division of the master bedroom into an en suite complete with power shower.

The house, no doubt, was revelling in its long overdue makeover. His wife was not.

I couldn't believe life could be so mundane and so, so uneventful. During the past year I had hardly deviated from the same old routes, excepting the occasional minor diversion to avoid an accident, outage at a set of traffic lights, or a spillage of some noxious fluid on the road.

It's not only drivers who get bored, you know. We cars thrive on variety and new places to discover.

Roger, with time to spare, had become Sylvia's personal taxi. She had managed to persuade old Mr Crooks to extend her hours to a full day from the half days she had worked for many years. It might have had something to do with the guilt he felt for getting rid of Roger, or more likely the soft spot he had always had for the strong-willed and well-organised woman with the striking green eyes.

Every day now for nigh on twelve months the workday routine had been the same. After seeing to Henry we set off for Fleesem's in the middle of Barchester. Barring any deviating events we would arrive outside Fleesem's main office some twenty-five minutes later, where Sylvia would be deposited on the pavement after the customary kiss and the 'See you later –

love you' response to the 'Have a good day' departing pleasantry. Then back home along the same route.

The ritual of shopping in Grevington on a Saturday afternoon was deeply ingrained. That never changed. Sundays had become a day to dread. Instead of going to the seaside as we used to do, or into the lovely countryside that this part of the world is famous for, I often found myself on the drive being cleaned by Roger. Yet again.

Now being washed and vacuumed once a week is delightful. Twice a week is tolerable. Five times a week is verging on the psychotic. Why Roger had slipped into the habit I can only guess. Since the initial false euphoria of escaping the world of regimented work, Roger had lapsed into a world of... regimented leisure. Part of his daily routine was to wash me all over, including my undersides; often with a hosepipe now the weather was improving. I was dry on the outside but, unbeknown to Roger, continuously wet or damp on the areas invisible to him. As a consequence my rusting joints began to tighten up, and many times in the early mornings I suffered from what we cars call an 'autoarthritic seizure'. I prayed the man would get a life, and leave me alone.

'You must be the cleanest car for miles around with him washing you every day,' teased Neville's latest car, a five-year-old Nissan Primera, after one particularly invigorating hose-down.

It was remarkable how Neville's personal transport had changed over the years as his ability to achieve sales targets had deteriorated. Ten years ago, Neville was the successful manager of a large sales team. He enjoyed all the trappings – generous base salary, fabulous bonus scheme, healthcare for him and his family, overseas incentive trips, and a prestigious Jaguar XJ6 with all the trimmings. Neville used to tease Roger about me, saying, 'Still got that old thing, Rog? About time you got shot, don't you think?' To which Roger invariably replied, drawing on his solid accountant's logic, 'There's no reason why I should, Neville. The car's never let me down, there's absolutely no depreciation, it gets me about, and frankly it simply does the job.'

Neville would only shake his head and wonder how anyone could be seen dead in a car that was over fifteen years old.

Then Neville, like Icarus, had his wings melted, not by the sun but by the heat of a thorough external audit which turned up some very interesting accounting practices in his company. In collusion with the finance director, Neville and his sales team had been recognising revenue for orders sold but not yet delivered, and this custom had been going on for several years. The sleight of hand made the current financial year's sales figures look great, and Neville and his team would swan off for a week to Bali, Mexico, Florida – or wherever the 'Top Achievers Club' was being held. All very well. Until some very large orders got cancelled in one particular financial year, and this became somewhat of a problem. The auditors doggedly latched on to this. Neville felt the heat all right. After the auditors reported their findings, the directors shifted the blame on to the shoulders of the finance director, who croaked on the sales team, and Neville took the hit. Goodbye finance director. Goodbye Neville. Goodbye Jaguar.

Six months later Neville was back in work as a salesman in a much smaller company. Not as a sales manager. Nobody would trust him to do that job again. The perks were still there – reasonable base salary and a tolerable bonus scheme. Healthcare for him and his family and overseas incentive trips had disappeared, never to reappear. In came the Renault Safrane.

The gradual slide into sales oblivion now started. Neville, although acknowledged as a motivating and competent (if a little dodgy) sales manager, found life as a salesman very different. Like many sales managers his rise from salesman to manager had been rapid, and like many sales managers hadn't been based on any proven success as a salesman. Life on the sales front line is tough. Neville found there was no hiding place. No opportunity to create fictitious sales, no room for sandbagging. His management saw to that.

In the first year Neville made 60 per cent of his target. A credible effort given he was building his pipeline. The next year he made 43 per cent and came under increased scrutiny. In his third and last year he scraped 28 per cent and earned himself a foreshortened disciplinary procedure and the gift of a P45. Out went the Renault.

Another six months on gardening leave during which Neville,

at his creative best, completely reinvented his now glowing CV and blagged his way through several interviews, narrowly missing out on the final cut. Then, in the last month of 1997, he struck lucky and got a sales position with an even smaller company, in a home-based role on a reasonable base salary and a small bonus scheme. Thanks to the ever predatory taxman, anyone who had a company car was now an easy victim to swell the Inland Revenue's coffers. Companies short-sightedly made the decision that it was in their salesmen's best interest if they provided their own transport, and to compensate they would offer a monthly car allowance. Taxable, of course. A three-year-old Citroën Xsara appeared on Neville's drive.

Tracey, his wife, got a job checking out at the Sainsbury's in Milverton.

Neville's job lasted three years. Expectations of him were not high in the company, and only once did he scrape 50 per cent of his target. The rot had well and truly set in. In career terms he'd hit rock bottom and found himself uninterested in his company, his customers and his work. Shortly after the millennium celebrations he threw in the towel, handed in his resignation and flogged the Citroën. He was without a car for the next six months until a Nissan Primera materialised.

The Primera was to be Neville's last car in his life in Comberton. For two years he survived by doing paid jobbing work and gardening in the daytime (without declaring it to the taxman), and taxi driving for a firm in Milverton in the evenings. Tracey meanwhile had been promoted from the tills to groceries supervisor.

'They've decided to move,' the Primera informed me. 'To somewhere called Whitby.'

This was a surprise. I hadn't heard Roger or Sylvia mention it, even though Roger often chatted with Neville if he saw him at home during the day. Mind you, Roger had become very uninterested in anything else except his own problems of late.

'No! When did you hear that?' I asked.

'Last night when I was bringing them back from the chip shop. I guess they must have been discussing it for some time as the conversation was all about seeing the estate agent and making an appointment with the solicitor. It sounded to me as if the decision had been made.'

'Didn't you have any idea?'

The Primera thought for a moment. 'I suppose looking back on it I might have put two and two together, and come up with four instead of the usual three. I did hear her saying she'd put in for a transfer. I thought she meant to Barchester.'

Primeras had a reputation for not being the sharpest knife in the drawer.

'Are you certain it's Whitby?'

'No, I mean, yes. I know they mean Whitby, because she said that's where she used to live when she was a child. Whitby. It would be pleasant to go back and see the old place, she said.'

This was a lot of thinking all at one go for the Primera. He lapsed into silence and I wondered if he'd regretted starting the conversation.

'I presume you'll be going with them?' I asked, after giving the Primera time to recharge his grey cells.

'I dunno. Suppose so. This is my third home and no one keeps me for long. I've got used to it.'

I had clearly touched a nerve.

It's a sad thing the way drivers behave towards cars nowadays, and the Primera was a case in point. Three different drivers in five years. Shameful.

We cars had so looked forward to the millennium, hoping the dawning of a new age would usher in a change of attitude in the way the drivers treated us. In the nineties they became very cavalier, and the most deeply respected rules of their *Highway Code* had been abused. Don't park on double yellow lines. They did. Signal when you are preparing to overtake. They didn't. Stop at a red light. They wouldn't. Be courteous to other road users. You must be joking.

The new dawn came and went with street parties and the biggest displays of fireworks ever seen. As with their bizarre custom of making and almost immediately breaking any New Year's resolution (we cars could never fathom this strange and pointless habit), the drivers slipped back into their old ways within days. That depressed us, but things couldn't get any worse. Or so we thought. Then along came easy credit.

We cars had the equivalent of a baby boom. Not long beforehand a driver had to stump up a third of the price of a car in ready cash as a deposit, and then if he or she wanted to spread the remaining cost he or she had to jump through a number of hoops to get finance. This kept our population growth steady. Then some tortured financial mind devised easy credit. Any driver who had a heartbeat had easy credit offered to them. The third down as a deposit flew out of the window, the financial hoops were rent asunder and scattered to the four winds. Drivers could now walk into a dealer, pick their brand new car, put down a pittance and pay the remainder over an extraordinarily long term. The intention was they would keep the car until the loan was paid off. They didn't, of course; they just changed the car part-way through, extended the loan term and carried on, often doing this several times.

The outcome was mind-boggling. The makers couldn't produce sufficient new cars to meet the demand created by easy credit, and only the old, astute or conservative bought used cars. The euphemistically titled 'pre-owned vehicle' market slumped. Why buy second-hand when you could buy new for next to nothing?

Easy credit will probably be recorded in history books as the last nail in the coffin of the Golden Days of Motoring.

The Primera got it right. Neville and Tracey upped sticks, downsized and moved back 'up north' to a much smaller but very pretty cottage on the outskirts of Whitby. We later learnt that Neville had taken up dog-walking full time. Tracey was promoted to store manager of the local Sainsbury's. Their careers had metamorphosed into each other.

In came Mr and Mrs Kumar. A cardiologist at the King Edward IV hospital in Barchester, Mr Kumar was an effusive, short, and rather rotund man with impeccable manners and a liking for a good malt whisky. Mrs Kumar had a similar nature and stature and a liking for a good cabernet sauvignon. The Kumar's children were all grown up and the last of them had flown the nest some years before their parents moved in next door. So Mr and Mrs Kumar rattled around in their palatial house, delighting in chatting with their new neighbours in Comberton, and throwing parties for their extended family, many of whom used to live in the depressed areas of Barchester and Grevington but had now migrated to the surrounding villages as they progressed upwards on the economic ladder.

Mr Kumar liked his cars. In keeping with his professional status he drove a Range Rover, though he could barely see over the steering wheel.

Roger liked the Kumars from the first day they moved in, and straight away came round to introduce themselves. Less than a week later they invited the Buntings around for 'tiffin' and delighted Roger with their harmless, if quirky, mixture of reserved 'Englishness' and brash 'Punjabiness'. This contrasted sharply with Neville and his flashy manner, and Tracey with her rather coarse sense of humour and Essex Girl ways.

However, Sylvia was more reserved. She didn't take to Mrs Kumar's eager friendliness, and her way of calling Sylvia 'Mrs Bunting, my dear'. Roger said she was being too critical and should take into account that English wasn't the Kumar's first language, and although they spoke it very well they 'lacked certain idioms' and spoke as if 'from a *Brush Up On Your English* book'. It wasn't to be criticised, or made fun of, and thank heavens for people with Mr Kumar's medical skills. God only knows what state the National Health Service would be in without them. He had arrived in an alien country with his young wife, raised a good family and contributed substantially to the world of work. This was a lot more than could be said for many of the native English.

'I can appreciate that but, well, they're so different,' she protested whenever he put in a good word for the Kumars.

'I must disagree with you, Sylv. How do you mean, different?' countered Roger. 'Granted, their diet may be a little different from ours, but there's nothing unusual in that. As an example, we don't survive on processed meat, rubbery cheese, doughy bread, crisps and pop like many people do. They may also have a garish choice of decor for our tastes, but there's much worse around than theirs. Take Sid Baxter at Number 15. In his house you'll find he's painted all the skirting boards purple! How tasteless is that?'

'It's the way she dresses that I find hard to take. Wearing a Sari. It's not right. If they're going to live in this country then they should dress like we do. She's been here long enough to know that. I think she does it just to get people talking about her. Mr Kumar wears western clothes all the time, so why can't she?' she pouted.

'Look darling, it's a silly argument really. If Mrs Kumar likes the traditional dress, then what's the harm in that? She's not causing distress to anyone. Just go along with it and ignore what she wears.'

'She'll be offering me a sari next,' glowered Sylvia.

'I wouldn't be surprised, she's that generous. You never know, a red one might just suit you.'

It was thanks to Mr Kumar that Roger was brought back into the world of the employed.

Returning one morning from a stroll to the local Spar to collect the latest *Build Your Own Conservatory* magazine, Roger spied Mr Kumar coming out of the Buntings' drive. He greeted Roger, all smiles, and told him that he'd been knocking on his front door but after a while guessed that Roger wasn't in.

'Lucky for you that I am not going out first thing,' stated Mr Kumar, wagging a podgy forefinger to and fro. 'I have a proposition for you. Oh, yes. A very interesting proposition indeed. Let us have a cup of tea. Mrs Kumar has the kettle on.'

Mrs Kumar was very discreet. She ushered her husband and Roger into the sitting room at the back of the large house. The rear views of the houses on this side of the road really were spectacular, overlooking open fields with the coombe stretched across the near horizon. It was a slightly different perspective than the Buntings' which was truncated by a dividing privet hedge between the neighbours, so they could not quite see the lower reaches of the coombe. Today the early morning sun was starting to throw a shimmering amber shadow against the wall of the room. It held the promise of an auspicious day.

'I am thinking it is two sugars, is it not Roger?' Mrs Kumar wheeled a gilded trolley in and brought it to a halt next to the coffee table that separated her husband and Roger. 'And maybe I could tempt you with a chocolate digestive?'

'Only one sugar please, Chitti. I've got to try to get rid of some of the midriff.' (Mrs Kumar's full name was Chitralekha – 'as beautiful as a picture' – but she'd condensed it to Chitti as her English friends seemed to struggle with the unabridged version.)

'So I am assuming no digestive, then?' teased Mrs Kumar.

'Oh, I'm taking things a little at a time. One's OK.'

She placed the teapot on the table and set out two lavishly decorated china cups. After pouring the tea she popped one spoonful of sugar into Roger's cup, and barely a half into her husband's. After giving her husband a conspiratorial wink, she grasped the trolley, navigated it around the edge of the room and exited with a, 'Now don't you be forgetting, Gagandeep. We are needing to be in Milverton to get our shopping before one o'clock.'

'Yes, yes, my dear. No problem,' called Mr Kumar to the disappearing sari and waved her away with his hand. 'Lovely woman, Mrs Kumar,' he whispered to Roger.

Standing up, he walked over to the window and gazed at the glowing sun as it started to heat the lush fields with its radiant warmth.

'You know, Roger. You and I are very fortunate. Yes, very fortunate indeed. My father would never have imagined living in a house as grand as this with such a view. I am proud to say that I gave him all that a Punjabi father could wish for in a son. Educated, successful, and respected by society.' He paused to clear his throat, and turned around to look at Roger. 'You are I are alike in some ways, Roger. We are both from good homes where there was very little spare money. We both married lovely ladies. We have good friends. But we are also quite different. Mrs Kumar and I were blessed with our children. I cannot imagine what life would be like without them. I also found a very worthwhile profession, one where hopefully' – he took a deep breath and let it slowly exhale – 'they would never make me… redundant.'

Roger felt a lump in his throat.

'I am going to be very honest with you, my friend,' Mr Kumar continued. 'I sense that you have – how should I put this – lost interest a little? I am thinking it is about time that you started earning a living again, is it not?'

Mr Kumar's bluntness shocked Roger, but he knew he was right. The job-hunting had nigh-on ceased completely, and any chances of an interview were, he knew, illusory. He continued to attend the Jobcentre out of habit, if only to register he was still alive. They didn't care. As long as he read the job adverts and wrote the occasional application he would still collect his Jobseekers' Allowance, the pittance it was. The racking his brain to think of ways to earn an income in self employment had also proved fruitless.

'Gagandeep, you're right, I know. It's just that, well, I've only ever known accountancy, and clearly I'm not cut out to be any kind of entrepreneur. I have tried but it's like staring into a dense fog. I just don't have any idea of how to go about earning money. It's not as if I have a trade I can fall back on, like a plumber or electrician. I'm an accountant, for God's sake. That's what I do. But nobody wants to employ a fifty-eight-year-old accountant nowadays, and I'd be out of touch with all the changes that have been going on in the past two years. I guess that's why I fill my time with doing jobs around the house. It passes the day.'

'And your life will pass before you know it, Roger. Before long you'll be an old man with the most beautiful home in Comberton,' he chuckled, lightening the tone of the conversation. 'That is why, on such a beautiful day as this, I have a proposition to put to you.'

Returning to his seat Mr Kumar took a large mouthful of tea and let the quenching fluid slip down his throat. He leaned forward.

'I have a second cousin called Sanjay Guntupalli. Are you familiar with the "Bill and Ben" garden centre chain?'

Roger wasn't sure. He thought the name did ring a bell.

'Last month Sanjay acquired the chain from its owners after quite a battle. It was in the *FT* at one point.'

Ah, that's where I know the name from, thought Roger.

'If you follow this kind of thing as I do if my family is involved, you may know that Bill and Ben also own a number of other garden centres. Whitticombe is one of them.'

Whitticombe Garden Centre was the largest garden centre in the area around Comberton, and it serviced all the local villages. A little run down, it was popular for its ease of access, plenty of parking spaces, and good selection of plants and shrubs. It was lacking in what is known as 'a shopping experience' however, and often potential customers would suffer the inconvenience of travelling to the much more stylish Greenfingers Centre on the outskirts of Milverton.

'You know, we Punjabis can be very focused in pursuit of our wants, and young Sanjay is definitely very focused. Very, very focused.' Pausing for effect, Mr Kumar turned to look out of the window once more. 'It's going to be a beautiful day, Roger. Oh yes, a very beautiful day. And a very fortunate one for you, I might add.'

'I'm sorry, Gagandeep, you've lost me.'

Once more the little man turned to address his guest. Once again he took another gulp of tea, which by now was almost lukewarm.

'It is so exciting, you see. So exciting. I—'

Just at that moment Mrs Kumar popped her head round the door.

'Have you asked him yet Gagi?'

'Not yet Chitti, my dear. I was just about to tell—'

'Well get on with it, man. It is almost time that we are going. Are you wanting another pot of tea?'

'No thank you, my dear. Now please let me get on with what I am saying!'

'Get to the point then, and don't keep the poor man in suspense.' Clucking, she again disappeared, this time closing the door firmly shut after her.

'Mrs Kumar is right. I do like to go on and on. It is my love of the English, you see? Such a colourful language. Anyway, what was I saying? Ah, yes, my second cousin Sanjay. Well, yesterday evening at the club – Sanjay's been elected as captain of the B Team you know – Sanjay revealed some of the plans he has for two of his new "non-Bill and Ben" garden centres. Whitticombe was one of them. "Cousin Gagi," he says, "it needs bringing into the twentieth century, never mind the twenty-first. It needs a clear out from top to bottom and some people with fire in their bellies putting in." He has such a way with the words, don't you think? "I've found a great chap to run the place and I'm looking for a solid financial controller whom I can trust, but they're not easy to come by." It took a little time for the switching on of the light in my head, but then I knew what I had to say to Sanjay. "Cousin," I said, "I think I may be able to help you. I know a top, top man. Currently between jobs but keen to take on new challenges. I would personally recommend him, and his credentials are impeccable. Should I ask him to get in touch with you?" "Cousin Gagi," says he, "you never cease to surprise me. Here's my card. Ask him to contact me asap. We need to get going. Time is money, eh?" "Exactly, Sanjay, that's what I always tell my private patients," I replied.'

'What are you saying, Gagandeep?'

'I am saying that if you play your cards right and with my personal recommendation, I have no doubt you will secure a position as the new financial controller of Whitticombe. What are you thinking of that, then?'

On reflection it hadn't really been an interview. More of a 'getting to know you' chat over a light lunch at the Barchester Hilton. Sanjay and his younger brother Dilip were charming, both in their mid-thirties, both university educated, both trained in the law, both very shrewd. The brothers (along with another younger brother, Monish) were beginning to build a sizeable retail empire from small beginnings as the owners of two minimarkets in Barchester. They had steadily and astutely grown their burgeoning empire from this humble beginning to the point where they were now of real worry to the large national retailers. Bill and Ben had been a shock to those in the City. To think that a couple of rookies could better the hard-nosed professionals was incredible. The coup had thrown the brothers (trading as Alhambra Group) into the media spotlight, and they had handled the pressure well. Now everybody was unsure where Alhambra Group might pop up next.

'I'm afraid Whitticombe and others like it are an anachronism,' concluded Sanjay, with Dilip nodding his agreement. 'All right, the business has been plodding along for years but it lacks appeal. For sure, people will pop in if they want a packet of seeds or the odd pot plant or pair of gardening gloves. We want to make it somewhere they can take their kids, enjoy a meal, and even have a day out. That's why we bought Bill and Ben – because we believe the formula there – although it needs tweaking – is what is demanded by the paying public. Look at the year-on-year figures.' He nodded to Dilip, who produced a lightweight laptop from its case beside his chair, cleared a space on the table for it, flipped open the lid, swiftly made a few keystrokes and swivelled it round to give Roger a view of the screen.

'This is Bill and Ben. Here,' indicated Sanjay, pointing at the screen, 'is where the new strategy began to kick in. And here,' moving his finger along an upwardly sloping blue line, 'is how that strategy has paid dividends over the past three years. Impressive, isn't it? But we can do more.' He made some swift keystrokes and opened another file on the laptop. 'Now this,' he continued, 'is Whitticombe.'

In sharp contrast to the previous steep incline, the screen showed a gradual decline. 'This is why we need to take some drastic action with the laggards we've picked up. We know they have the potential with the correct management and investment to bring up the performance to that of Bill and Ben. We don't want to brand them as Bill and Ben but give them more of an independent, family-owned feel. We need to get it right. So we've decided that Whitticombe will be the one to try our ideas out on in the hope it will be a model for the others.'

For the first time in a long, long time Roger felt genuinely excited. He stared at the graphs and figures that danced in front of his eyes on the TFT screen. His accountant's brain was processing as it hadn't done for almost two years – absorbing, dissecting, analysing, reorganising. Even at a first glance he was able to see the stark comparison between Whitticombe and Bill and Ben. Even the cost profile of the former left a vast scope for improvement.

Dilip brought his attention back to the conversation.

'We've offered positions to a new Whitticombe team. All we're missing is the financial controller.'

Sweat broke out on Roger's palms and he felt a prickly heat at the base of his neck. 'This is it, then,' he thought. 'They've shown me the sweet shop, now they'll probably take it away.'

'Tell us a little about you,' invited Sanjay.

So he did. For the next half hour he described his time at Robsem, Fleesem and Crooks, detailing his expertise, the clients he had worked with, the value he had brought to those clients. His position, salary, and anticipated prospects. It was a salutary experience. He had never considered just how much he had done for the firm until he had to condense it into just thirty minutes in front of two strangers.

'That's about it. Of course, the past two years—'

'Thanks, Mr Bunting,' interrupted Sanjay. 'Would you mind excusing my brother and me for a few minutes?'

'No, that's OK.' I've blown it.

After five tortuous minutes they returned but did not sit down. Holding out his hand, Sanjay grasped Roger's clammy paw and shook it with a slight nod of his head. Dilip followed suit.

'Sorry, but we must rush. We have an important meeting to attend. It was very nice meeting you. Very interesting to hear about yourself.' They turned in unison, and Roger felt his heart sink. After two steps Sanjay turned round.

'Oh yes, I should have said. We always take notice of what cousin Gagi tells us. You come very highly recommended. I shall ask my secretary to draft your offer letter tomorrow. I know you will find the terms acceptable. We do hope you join us. If you do, then you will find these are exciting times with Alhambra. Goodbye, Mr Bunting.'

Roger was left to pay the bill. He couldn't have cared less.

A hubbub of activity was taking place within the mock-Victorian archway that formed the main entrance to Whitticombe. Sounds of voices echoed around the interior of the large main building. There was a crackling of electricity in the air.

Whitticombe Garden Centre was having a makeover, and Roger Bunting was in the thick of things. His first six months as the newly installed Financial Controller of the garden centre had flown by.

When, on Saturday morning after his interview, his offer letter dropped through the letterbox exactly as the Guntupalli brothers said it would, he plucked it off the mat, tore open the envelope and carefully scrutinised the contents. At first he couldn't believe the generosity of their terms. They had clearly taken into consideration his previous status and made a good estimate of the salary he would have earned there. There was even a profit-sharing incentive, just like Fleesem's, only much more attractive if he met Alhambra's financial goals. Whooping with delight – a rare thing – he immediately shot out of the house, surprised the Kumars who were having a leisurely breakfast, hugged an unruly-haired Mr Kumar, and pecked a startled Mrs Kumar on the cheek. Waving the letter at them he thanked Mr Kumar profusely, declined a cup of tea, and rushed back home just in time to see a puzzled Sylvia staring at Mr Kumar, who was now standing on his front doorstep, resplendent in his red, blue and yellow dressing gown with his thumb stuck high in the air.

Ten minutes later the Buntings were waltzing around the kitchen, all caution to the wind. Normal service was to be resumed.

And resumed it had been. Once more Sylvia reduced her hours and went back to the old routine of afternoon working at Fleesem's. Roger installed himself in the rather antiquated offices of the garden centre, and, once introduced to the new management team and the staff, set about unravelling Whitticombe's financial mysteries.

It didn't take too long given his expertise. Fortunately, Whitticombe kept clear, computerised financial records, and within a week Roger felt he had a sufficient grasp of the financials to present to the rest of the management team during his first review with them and the Guntupallis. All were impressed with his quick grasp of the situation, and the initial list of suggestions he made for certain cost efficiencies that could be implemented without affecting the running of the operation.

There was exciting news for the team at the next meeting. Tam Browne, Whitticombe's Chief Executive, returned from his regular review with the Guntupallis and announced that the decision had been taken to execute the plan for a complete makeover for the centre. This was a major investment and showed the Guntupallis' faith in the strategy and plans of the management team. Plans were to be put in hand immediately for the appointment of architects.

Roger was intimately involved throughout the whole process, from appointment of architects, consideration of alternative schemes, costing implications, preparation of tender for building and refurbishment work, evaluation of tenders, and award of contract. He absolutely revelled in every aspect of the project. Now that the work was finally under way, he enjoyed walking round the progressing works with Tam, the architect, and the contractor's site manager.

He had found his way back to the Land of the Living.

Diwali (2004)

Diwali. A very unusual word, and one that I was introduced to only recently.

It was while we were parked on our drives one day that the Range Rover and I started chatting about our drivers, as we often did. He was fast learning about Indian ways and habits. Although the Kumars cultivated their 'Englishness' very well, behind closed doors they were really very traditional and were keen to maintain the ways of the old country, he told me.

'It'll be Diwali soon,' he mused.

'Diwali, what's that?' I asked him. It was a word I'd never come across in my twenty-eight years on the road.

'It's fantastic,' he answered. 'It's one of the biggest Hindu festivals. They celebrate for five continuous days, with the third day being a special "Festival of Lights". The Kumars light candles all around their house. And the number of fireworks Mr Kumar lets off! He's crazy about fireworks. Puts Guy Fawkes to shame! You'll really enjoy it. All his relatives will be there. Wait till you meet some of the cars! There'll be some exotic types there, I can tell you. Ferraris, Maseratis, Lamborghinis. Those Italians always have some juicy tales to tell about their drivers!'

The mention of the Italians brought back happy memories of days gone by with the Conrad Quinney set. I couldn't wait.

'Hi, Roger, how's things?'

Roger looked up from the drive, where he was on his hands and knees studiously pulling out tiny weeds from between the block paving using an ancient pair of tweezers. Beaming over the dense privet hedge at him was the upper two-thirds of the chubby, moustachioed face of Mr Kumar. Atop his head was a yellow and black baseball cap, with the word CAT emblazoned across the front.

'Hello, Gagandeep. Fine thanks. Just doing a bit of weeding before the weather gets too bad.'

'Goodness gracious, terrible job. I don't know why we redid our drive. Much less trouble when the blasted thing was tarmac. I am correct in thinking you're regretting it also?'

'You know how it goes. Seemed like a good idea at the time.'

'Yes. My thinking as well. Why don't you get someone to do it for you? My nephew Ranjeet has a landscaping business. I could get him to send one of his boys around if you wish. Very cheap, very good.'

'Very kind of you, but I find it quite therapeutic, thanks. Off to the club again?'

'Oh yes, I am going there right now. But before I go Mrs Kumar has asked me not to forget to invite you to the party we are having. For Diwali.'

The 'club' was the latest rung climbed on the social ladder of Mr Kumar. Proposed by the current captain – one Graham Chowdhury, another distant relative – and seconded by Messrs Ronnie Ghoshdashtidar and Kenny Ramamurthy, he had recently applied for and been accepted into the once unassailable fortress that was the Royal Barchester Golf Club. No mean achievement, it may be said, as somehow he had managed to go from applicant to full member in less than six months. It usually took at least eighteen. Mr Kumar had very influential friends, including of course the Guntupallis.

'Who's Diwali? Is he a relative of yours?' It seemed as good a guess as any to Roger who had stood up and walked over to the dividing hedge in order to see more of his neighbour's face. I wasn't alone in my ignorance of the word.

There was a chortle from the newly initiated member. 'Oh no, it is not a person, it is a festival. A very important one. And it will be a very special party we are having!' He wagged his finger at Roger. 'Mrs Kumar has told me that she will not take "no" from Mrs Bunting for an answer. And what Mrs Kumar wants, Mrs Kumar gets,' he stated, rolling his eyes and chortling.

Comberton was changing, and changing fast. It started in Barchester as it always did, and slowly but surely spread out like an ink stain to the surrounding smaller towns and villages. The first signs were noticed not long after the countries of Estonia, Latvia, Lithuania, Poland, Slovakia, Slovenia and the Czech Republic were permitted entry to the European Union. Barchester had always had a small Polish community, going back as far as the days of the Second World War. They had integrated reasonably well, although the first generation still stuck to the ways of the old country and kept a Polish Club running. This didn't harm anyone and no one worried much about either the club or the Poles. People liked them, and they in turn liked Barchester.

Then, in 2004, things began to change. Almost overnight many strange, guttural accents were heard on the streets and in the cafés and pubs of Barchester. Not just the odd person or two, but whole family groupings. Children and mothers wearing headscarves; fathers with swarthy complexions and grey stubble faces. On a busy Saturday it was as if the town had been invaded. This may have gone without remark had it not been for the fact that, wherever you were, within five minutes of being there some woman with her brood in tow would try to sell you something. In the end it became a nuisance and the people of Barchester began to lose patience.

Of course, ignorance laid the blame at the Poles' feet. People weren't astute enough to distinguish Polish from Slovak, Slovenian, Czech or any other Eastern European tongue. They simply branded them as 'Poles'.

The Poles didn't like the sudden unwanted attention they were beginning to receive. They'd lived quite happily in Barchester for the past sixty years, peacefully going about their business. They weren't about to let the newly 'Unionised' immigrants spoil things for them. A turf war ensued, one from which the entrenched Poles were to come out on top. This forced the newcomers out into the outlying smaller towns and villages, where normally they would have been unable to settle owing to the high property prices.

However, fortune was to smile on them in an unexpected way. Since the turn of the millennium there had been a rocketing interest in buying properties as an investment, owing to underperforming, and in some cases criminal, pension providers. The British public had been seduced into believing that 'Buy to Let' was the way to monetary nirvana. This led to a buying spree not only in Barchester but in the feeder towns and villages surrounding it. Now there were plenty of properties available to rent. The new wave of immigrants sussed that this was the way in. A popular trick was for one family to sign up for a short-term tenancy, and then on the quiet move another half-dozen-or-so relatives into the property.

Nobody ever checked. If the owner employed a management agent, the agent rarely, if ever, visited the property. If the owner managed the property himself, they only visited if requested by the tenant. Which, in most cases, was never. Communities of Eastern Europeans began to spring up all around the county town of Barchester.

Ken Mansell, Mr Kumar's neighbour on the opposite side to the Buntings, lost his wife to cancer in October 2003. In his mid-seventies, he had been persuaded by his daughter to go and live with them in the nearby village of Lower Mortmain. The daughter, keen to keep her legacy, had persuaded her father that it would be in his best interests to keep the house and 'make a killing' by letting it out. Ken agreed. Within two weeks of the house being put up for let, a well-presented Slovenian man had signed the short-lease tenancy agreement at the managing agents and moved in. After one week in occupation the man was never seen again, and two much less presentable men and a woman appeared. Gradually the number of persons occupying the house swelled from three to a number that could never be accounted for accurately owing to the continual comings and goings, but estimated (by Mr Kumar) to be around the dozen mark. Talking, shouting, laughing, and the sound of strange music regularly filled the Kumars' evenings well into the early hours.

Normally the most placid of men, Mr Kumar merely tut-tutted as he sat and watched his favourite TV shows or recalled the day's incidents with his wife. The Kumars were patient people. Usually. But after a while the continuous racket finally got to them. One Saturday evening two weeks before Diwali, Mr Kumar got up from his chair, shook his head at Mrs Kumar, and walked around to Ken's house. After pressing the front door bell three times he was confronted by a large, pockmarked, bald-headed man, covered in tattoos and wearing a grimy vest and smoking a cheroot.

'You want?' asked the man, blowing a cloud of acrid grey smoke which lingered in the air just above Mr Kumar's head.

'Excuse me, but do you mind making a little less noise? I am having a little difficulty listening to my television.'

'We party,' returned the man, as if that was all the explanation that was necessary.

'Yes, but I am having a problem with all the noise you are making,' persisted Mr Kumar.

'Is too bad,' the smoker countered, directing another lungful of smoke on a more downward trajectory, straight into the face of Mr Kumar.

'Yes, but—' Mr Kumar protested as the door was shut firmly in his face.

Unsettled by the abrupt manner of the man but determined not to be fobbed off, Mr Kumar pressed the doorbell again. On the fifth or sixth ding-dong the door opened and the lout reappeared.

'Look here,' started Mr Kumar. 'I am being a reasonable man—'

'Is party. You go fuck.' With that the door was again slammed shut in the little man's startled face.

Fuming, Mr Kumar marched home and headed straight for the phone.

'Emergency services? Yes, yes, police please,' he piped into the mouthpiece as a nervous Mrs Kumar watched him from the kitchen.

'Yes, sir. Can I be of assistance?' asked a bass voice.

'Yes, yes. I am calling as it is a complaint I am making.'

'I'm sorry, sir. This line is for emergency services. Please call your local police station.'

'Oh, yes. Sorry, sorry.'

'What's the number for the local police, Chitti?'

'Wait a minute, Gagi. Ah, yes, here I have it. 01654 760000.'

Ring ring. Ring ring. Ring ring.

'Hello, Milverton Police Station. Can I help you?'

'Yes. I am calling as it is a complaint I am making.'

'Your name and address please, sir?'

'Gagandeep Kumar. Mr Gagandeep Kumar, 18 Granville Crescent, Comberton.'

'And what is the exact nature of your complaint, sir?'

'I am suffering from antisocial neighbours and one of them has just sworn at me! The noise is going all day and night and my wife and I are going round the bend! Can you send someone down to tell them to please be quiet?'

'Were you threatened in any way, sir?'

'The appearance of the man was threatening! All muscles and a shaven head! Like something from Genghis Khan!'

'I'm sorry sir, but we can't caution somebody for the way they look otherwise we'd do nothing else with our scarce resources. Have any other neighbours complained?'

'No, but I am living much closer than anyone else. It is me who is having the big problem. They're from Eastern Europe you know, probably illegals.'

'If that's the case, sir, I'd suggest you contact the Immigration Office. We have our hands tied, you see. Plus all the paperwork. You just can't imagine what it's like to be a policeman nowadays.'

'It is really that bad, is it?'

'Mr Kumar, you can't imagine even in your wildest dreams. What with the battle against the drug business, youths drinking alcohol on the streets and behaving like packs of wild dogs – and that's just the girls. Now we've got a massive illegal cigarette trade. But you know the worst of this job, sir?'

'No, no. Do tell me.'

'The paperwork. You would not believe the paperwork.'

'Oh, yes I would. It is a growing problem for me also. All these bloody government targets. It is an outrage!'

'Then you can sympathise with the poor plod, sir. No wonder we don't have the time to pursue the real criminals any more. We've got to have a life as well, you know. We're just ordinary people like you.'

'Well, when you are putting it like that—'

'Exactly, sir. Thank you for your understanding. Is that all? I must get on. Things to do, things to do.'

'Well, I—' Click.

'What did they say, Gagi? Are they sending someone around to stop the noise?'

Mr Kumar just gawked at her, a look of utter amazement on his face.

It had been one of Mr Kumar's best-ever Diwali parties. His friends and relatives had turned up in droves. The Kumar's get-togethers were prestigious events and it was quite something if you were invited to them. So it was quite an honour for a non-Indian couple such as Roger and Sylvia to receive an invitation.

Hesitant at first, Sylvia had been unsure whether to accept the invitation. It was only on Roger's pleading that she finally agreed to go along, with the proviso that if she wasn't enjoying it they would make their excuses and retire early.

It had worked out much better than expected. The Indian ladies had fussed over her flowing mane and marvelled at her green eyes, and she'd had very interesting conversations with several of the very well-educated Indian men, particularly Ronnie Ghoshdashtidar and Kenny Ramamurthy, both educated at Oxford, both stockbrokers, and both upright committee members at Mr Kumar's golf club. It was no disadvantage that they were also both good-looking and extremely charming.

Roger had been taken under Mr Kumar's wing and introduced, in Mr Kumar's words, 'to everyone who mattered'.

When the singing and dancing began they found themselves drawn in, and, losing all self-consciousness (the alcohol contributed in no small way) they twirled and whirled with the best of them, Sylvia cutting a striking figure with her flowing locks streaming in a lustrous wave as she pirouetted around the Kumar's hallway.

Finally, exhausted and filled to the brim from Mrs Kumar's abundant buffet they said their 'thank yous', waved everybody goodbye and returned to the stillness of Hazlemere, with the animated sounds of the party ringing in their ears.

There was a rapid knocking on the front door. On opening it, Roger found an agitated Mr Kumar standing on the doorstep, forefinger wagging in the air.

'It is bloody well outrageous!' screamed Mr Kumar at Roger, eyes rolling to the heavens. 'Bloody well outrageous!'

'Dear me, Gagandeep, whatever is the matter? Do come in,' invited Roger, steering the worked-up chap into the kitchen.

'It is those bloody immigrants!' whooped Mr Kumar, wiping a sweating forehead with his pink silk handkerchief. 'Coming into our country! Who do they think they are?' With that he shrugged his shoulders and looked appealingly at Roger as if expecting an answer to his question.

It didn't take long for Roger to figure out exactly which 'bloody immigrants' Mr Kumar was referring to. Of late, his neighbours seemed to be the only thing that Mr Kumar thought about. The little man's customary good humour seemed to have vanished into thin air. All he ever talked about was the 'bloody immigrants' who lived next door.

'I'll make a cup of tea. You can tell me all about it.'

But Mr Kumar was not to be placated so easily. 'Who do they think they are, these Slovenians? Bloody upstarts, that's what they are! They come here in their thousands, milk the system and expect the same rights as everyone else. The only thing they won't do is work, the lazy devils! A curse on them!'

'Calm down Gagandeep, please. You'll do yourself an injury.'

'It won't be me who'll be getting an injury – it'll be those bloody immigrants! I tell you Roger, I've had it up to here. Up to here! Of all the bloody cheek! Do you know what happened this morning?'

Settling himself on the kitchen chair, Roger motioned Mr Kumar to do the same.

'Tell me.'

'At precisely seven thirty this morning when Mrs Kumar and I were fast asleep there was a very loud and persistent knocking on our door. We tried to ignore it at first but then it is getting even louder. "You'd better go, Gagi," says Mrs Kumar, "it's probably the milkman." So I quickly look out of the window, as I don't want to be mugged before breakfast, and what do I see? A police car parked on the road and two policemen at my door. "Oh, God," I thought to myself, "there's been a smash up on the motorway and they are coming to give me a fast escort to the hospital." All hands to the pumps, as they say.'

Sipping his tea he continued, 'So I am shooting down the stairs and opening the door. "Is it a very bad accident?" I ask. "If so I will dress immediately and be with you in ten minutes." The tallest of the policemen is looking at me as if I am Martian and is totally ignoring what I am saying. "Mr Kumar, Mr Gagandeep Kumar? Is that you, sir?" he is asking. "Yes, yes, that's me." "We've had a very serious complaint," he continues. "A complaint?" I am now very puzzled. "A complaint, sir. A complaint about excessive noise, coarseness, violence and even damage to property ensuing from activities in this house, sir."

'Now I am really beginning to worry. "When was this?" I am asking. "Last night, sir." "Last night? But last night was Diwali, don't you see?" I am thinking this knowledge will make everything clear. "Doesn't matter to me if it was the Queen's birthday, sir. A complaint is a complaint and we take it seriously. May we step in for a moment, please?" "Wait a minute," I protest. "Who is making this complaint?" "We're not at liberty to divulge that, sir. Now, are you going to let us in?" As I opened to door wider I looked past them and you know who I am seeing? I am seeing a dozen or so of those bloody immigrants on the front lawn next door smiling and waving at me!'

'Big trouble, huh, eh boyz?' asked the stranger, parked at an odd angle half on, and half off the kerb.

The Range Rover and I looked at each other. Then towards the battered old Skoda with his dark-ringed headlights and rusty grey wheels.

'Your driver don't mess with Praptotniks. They big trouble. Now he got problem. They bad family.'

The Range Rover was the first to speak.

'Sorry, I didn't catch your name?'

'Stefan they call me. Don't ask me why 'cos I not know. I been with Praptotniks long time. Long time in old country.'

'I'm Dolly,' I introduced myself.

'And I'm Ranjit, or that's what my driver calls me,' continued the Range Rover. 'I suppose it sounds to them like Rangee. Rangee Rover if you see what I mean.'

The Skoda chortled. 'That very funny. But you,' he nodded at me. 'Dolly? That girl name ain't it?'

I wish I had a pound for every time I'd heard that in the past thirty years. By now I would have been a car millionaire. Not that there was such a thing as a car millionaire.

'It may be a girl's name but it's also a nickname. It's Dolomite really. That's what I am.'

'You named after mountains? Cool.' said the Skoda.

Until then I never knew there was a mountain called Dolomite. 'Mount Dolomite? I've never heard of it.'

'Nor me,' added the Range Rover.

'Is no mountain. Is many mountains near old country. Very tall. Very dangerous. An' I never hear of car called Dolomite. How old you?'

It was a question I was frequently asked. My answer usually met with either astonishment or sympathy.

'Thirty next birthday.'

'Nemogoče! In old country nobody live that long! You look good for age! But why named after mountain?'

It wasn't something anyone had ever asked. 'I don't know. But I'm not just a Dolomite – I'm a Dolomite Sprint.'

Stefan looked at me, puzzled. 'Sprint. What this word mean?' he asked.

'It's a verb meaning to run. Or it could be a noun meaning a race.'

'Running mountain? Now Stefan is really confused.'

The thread was broken by the Range Rover. 'Look… Stefan. I'm a little worried what you said about the… the… Prap… Prap…'

'Praptotniks?' prompted the Skoda.

'Yes. Them.'

'Very bad Praptotniks. Very bad.'

'In what way?' I asked, intrigued.

Seeing that the police car was now taking notice of him, he lowered his voice.

'Listen me. I tell you.'

'But, officer, it is Diwali. It is a celebration. I will explain it to you.'

Poor Mrs Kumar stood next to her husband, wringing her

hands as he tried to explain the significance of Diwali, and what it meant to Hindus. The policeman listened patiently, but clearly had his own fixed idea of what had taken place. The intricacies and rites of Diwali were an information overload at this time of the day. Mr Kumar was cut short on his educating travels.

'Shall I tell you what I think, sir? I think you all had just a little too much to drink and let things get a little out of hand. Let's face it, it easily happens.'

'But we were not that loud!' protested Mr Kumar.

Unbuttoning the top breast pocket of his jacket, the policeman took out a black notebook and flipped open the pages.

'Let, me see. Ah, yes. Here we are: 23.27 first complaint registered. Excessive noise from 18 Granville Crescent. 23.42 second complaint. Coarse language heard from 18 Granville Crescent. 23.56 complaint. Shouting between man and woman at 18 Granville Crescent. Sounded like argument. 00.01. Ear-splitting noise as fireworks let off at 18 Granville Crescent. 00.08 firework nearly blinds child at house in Granville Crescent. 01.12 fireworks still going off at 18 Granville Crescent. Shall I go on, Sir?'

Slumping forward in his chair, Mr Kumar shook his head slowly from side to side. Mrs Kumar took the only course of action she knew.

'Would anyone like a cup of tea?'

The two policemen perked up. The call-out had meant the regulation morning cuppa in the station cafe had had to be abandoned.

'Two sugars, milk.'

'No sugar, milk. Now sir, as I was saying. This was not just one individual making a complaint. It was a whole series of call-ins. We take this kind of thing very seriously.'

'These complaints, were they in Eastern European voices, by any chance?' asked Mr Kumar, with a resigned look on his face.

'What are you implying, sir?'

'I am not implying anything. I am merely asking a question.'

'I'd be very careful, sir, if I was you. It may be construed that you are making a racially prejudiced slur. We take that very seriously, too.'

'I do not give a—' started Mr Kumar, losing his patience.

An impending disaster was saved by a quick-witted Mrs Kumar.

'Do you like a slice of Madeira cake with your tea, officers?'

'Mrs Kumar and I are considering moving. We are even thinking of returning to Chandigarh. India is changing, Roger. New opportunities are opening up all the time. Do you know I can now earn as much in India as I can in Barchester? And the cost of living is much lower. It is very tempting, very tempting indeed. Why, I even hear there is a credit experiment planned for Mumbai. '

'But all your family is here, Gagi. Your children all grew up here. You won't want to go back without them, surely?'

'Oh, no. I am discussing it with all the family. It is not just the bloody immigrants, Roger. It is a whole lot of things. The rotten NHS, the confused education system, the lack of respect for people, the selfish culture. No, the country is going to the dogs. And Mrs Kumar and I think we no longer want to be a part of it. My sons and daughters will make their own choices. But I do not want to grow old in a country full of layabouts and bloody immigrants. It is time for change. It is time for change.'

Out to Pasture (2005)

One day they were there, the next they were gone, removing every fixture and fitting from Ken's house. Nobody heard a thing. Not even the garages. You had to admit, the Praptotniks were good at what they did. Though what they did wasn't good. It was the talk of Comberton for weeks. Nothing as exciting as this had happened in the village for years; not since Bert McMahon had trashed the local grocer's Mercedes with his JCB, on discovering the Lothario had been liberally handing out orgasms to his beloved sixteen-year-old daughter.

One consequence was that the Kumars wavered in their plans for a return to the mother country. On revealing his intention to resign his post at the King Edward IV, Mr Kumar was offered a pay rise to encourage him to stay. Mrs Kumar was invited to join the committee of her local WI. They finally abandoned the idea when Mr Kumar was persuaded to be Social Secretary of the Barchester Royal.

'I am not understanding it, Roger. One minute all noise and trouble. The next, poof! Gone. I wonder what it is that made them go?'

The Range Rover and I knew. Thanks to Stefan the Skoda.

Unfortunately I can't reveal what he told us, as much as I'm tempted to. Rule 5: Never reveal secrets to any driver. They will twist what you tell them and use it against you to their advantage and your dismay.

I feel the weight of old age telling on me, now that 2005 is nearly over. It's been an eventful year. In March Roger celebrated his sixtieth birthday and was promoted to Chief Executive of Whitticombe on the retirement of Tam Browne. This was followed in May by Sylvia deciding to invent a new milestone in the marriage calendar – the celebration of thirty-one years of marriage – by planning a grand tour of Charente-Maritime.

I know what you're thinking. You're thinking, isn't it a bit dodgy taking a thirty-year-old car all that way? And you'd be right. The past three years have been very difficult for me as I've suffered from worn piston rings (necessitating a very costly engine rebuild), broken rear coil spring, two replacement constant velocity joints (my how they'd ached), broken windscreen, fractured fuel pipe and heater rebuild. It certainly isn't any fun getting old!

So I remained in the garage while they flew to France and hired one of the foreign makes for 'le grand tour'.

I really was glad of the rest.

'You know, Gagandeep, when we were in France we hired one of those new Peugeot 407s. Very impressive. Very impressive indeed. I didn't realise how much technology has progressed since we bought the Sprint.'

'How long are you having the old banger, Roger? I have not seen one of those on the road for, what... it must be at least ten years. Yours might be the only one left.'

'Let me see. We bought it in 1975. By gosh, doesn't time fly?'

'Thirty years old! Is it not about time to retire the old chap? Put him out to pasture so to speak? I would think you have definitely had your money's worth.'

'Funny you should say that. It's just what Sylvia and I have been thinking. It's been a great car but things have definitely started to go wrong over the past few years. The problem is finding the replacement parts – they're getting rarer and rarer. We've decided we need a change. We're going to sell the Sprint and buy one of those 407s. Everyone says diesel's the way to go, so we're doing our bit for the planet, too.'

No, I must have misheard. Selling me? No, never. We've been together nearly thirty years. I'd never known any driver other than Roger. Was my hearing failing, too?

'I am thinking you will not get much money for it. It is probably best just to scrap it. You might get twenty pounds if you are lucky.'

'Oh no, I couldn't do that. The car's been more like a friend all these years. Like a member of the family. And you'd be surprised just how much some folks would pay to get their hands on one of these. I've done some research on the Web and I'm going to advertise it in one of those collectors' magazines.'

So I was advertised for sale in *Collectors' Cars*, September 2005 edition. Yes, Roger did me proud, using his photographic skills to capture me at my finest; newly washed, waxed, vacuumed, and polished, set off with the Old Mill at Tottiecombe in the background to add some rustic charm.

But photos of cars don't reveal how sad we can be.

'That's it… over there. Strawberry Lane.' Sylvia poked a perfectly manicured crimson fingernail in the direction of a narrow lane, gently ascending from the apex of a sharp bend in the main road.

'I see it. Must say, this is rather a pleasant area. Very quiet and off the beaten track,' commented Roger. 'Come on, old girl [Roger had started calling me this rather infuriating name about five years ago]. Let's see what your new home's like.'

The lane wound itself around the base of a small, wooded hill, and rose gently for about 200 yards before the first of the houses came into view. The properties were unprepossessing, mostly made up of 1950s semis with the occasional detached bungalow sprinkled among them. There was no sign of any children, even though it was mid-morning on a Saturday. Judging by the external condition of the properties and lack of kids I guessed most of the occupants would be in middle age or older.

'What number are we looking for, Sylv?'

'Seventy-nine. I can see… yes, there's forty-nine. Keep going, it can't be too far.'

The dwellings were mostly bungalows now, with the semis fading away. They were also larger than lower down the lane, set much further back, and screened by either hawthorn or privet hedges.

'Look, there's a number on the gatepost,' said Sylvia. 'Yes, it's seventy-nine. This is the one.'

Roger slowly turned the wheel and glided on to the grassy verge running parallel to the hedge. 'Big day, old girl,' he whispered to me as he switched off my ignition. Stepping out, he closed my door, locked it, patted my roof and set off down the drive of Number 79 with Sylvia.

Big day.

Knock, knock.

No answer.

Knock, knock.

The door opened slowly to reveal a small, suntanned, white-haired man, dressed in an oversized fawn cardigan, grey crumpled trousers, and wearing Burberry carpet slippers.

'Yes, can I help you?' he asked.

'Mr Smallbone?' enquired Roger.

'Yes, that's me.'

'I'm Roger, Roger Bunting. We spoke earlier in the week. This is my wife, Sylvia. We've come to show you the car, as agreed. The Dolomite Sprint.'

'Ah, yes. Please do come in.' The white-haired man opened the door to reveal a hallway covered with display cases containing miniature models of buses – double deckers in reds, creams, and greens, and coaches in blues, yellows, and browns.

'I say, these are fascinating.' Roger was immediately glued to the displays, eyes scanning the names, companies and routes painted in precise script on cards next to the tiny models.

'Oh, yes they are. I've been collecting them for a very long time. Probably the finest collection in the country, so I've been told. They're all there – AEC, Dennis, Leyland, Bristol, Alexander – you name it, I've got it.' The white-haired man beamed with pride. 'I've got some that I'm restoring in the second bedroom, would you like to take a look?'

'Yes, pl—' Roger was cut off in mid sentence.

'Perhaps another time, Mr Smallbone. We're on a tight schedule and don't have a lot of spare time today. Now about the car...' Sylvia had taken command, bringing the two adolescently minded men to heel.

'Ah, yes, yes. I'm sorry, rude of me,' apologised Mr Smallbone. 'Would you like a cup of tea?'

'That's very kind of you, but as I said we're on a tight schedule. Another time maybe. Now, about the car...' Sylvia conducted herself into a spacious lounge looking out on to a rather unkempt front lawn, and settled herself into an overstuffed, chintz-covered armchair. The men settled themselves opposite her, Mr Smallbone on an identical armchair, Roger on the sofa.

'I'm a collector of all things to do with old vehicles, as you can see.' He swept his arm around the room to demonstrate the point. On the walls were photographs of old cars, some in black-and-white, many in colour, and an odd one or two in sepia. Every available horizontal surface was covered with creased and discoloured magazines, faded, yellow papers, and scale models – mostly of buses but also a number of cars.

'I've been doing this for... let me see... I'm eighty-five now... amazing how time flies... over sixty years. Ever since I rebuilt my first car. A 1937 Hillman Minx Deluxe.'

'My uncle had one of those! I remember the front wing falling off in town one day and he had to nip into Woolworth's, buy a ball of string, and tie it back on!' chimed in Roger, animatedly.

'Yes, they were prone to that,' agreed Mr Smallbone, nodding his head sagely. 'So when I noticed your advert in the paper selling the Sprint I decided that it would complement my collection of cars – two from every decade between 1930 and 2000. The Dolomite's now quite rare, but the Sprint is almost impossible to find. So I knew I had to have it, and that's why I telephoned you straight away and said as long as the condition was acceptable to me I would buy it. I'm so pleased you were able to bring it here. As I explained to you, I am no longer able to drive. Prone to epileptic fits, you see.' He raised his eyes and turned his palms skywards as if in apology.

'We discussed it and agreed it would only go to a good home,' Sylvia pointed out. 'That's the main reason we decided to come. It wouldn't do to be traipsing all over the country, Mr Smallbone, would it?'

'No, no, I don't suppose it would. I think you'll find the car will have an excellent home here of course. I am particular – very particular about the way I treat my charges.'

Charges. Roger liked that. He immediately felt a certain affinity for the old man.

'So, shall we show you the car?' asked Sylvia.

'I can't wait. I do admit I have seen a number over the past few years but unfortunately none has come up to my exacting standards,' explained Mr Smallbone, a rueful look on his face.

'Wonderful, Mr Bunting. Absolutely wonderful. I must say it's a very fine example of the marque. Rarely have I seen a thirty-year-old car in such excellent condition.' The old man tore the cheque out of its book, blew on the ink to dry it and handed it to Roger. 'I think it will probably be the jewel in the crown of my collection.'

'Thank you, Mr Smallbone.' Roger took the cheque, pulled out his wallet from his inside jacket pocket, folded the chair in half, placed it in the wallet and returned the wallet to the pocket. 'Might I ask you a small favour?'

'Certainly. What it is?'

'I would be absolutely delighted if you would take the time to show me your collection. I've always wondered what it would be like to see old cars from across the years.'

'Not old, Mr Bunting. I prefer "retired".'

'Roger, we—' Sylvia shot her husband an impatient look and started to rise from the chair on which she had been sitting while the men sorted out the financial arrangements, and the cheque-signing ceremony was completed. She was cut short.

'No, Sylvia. We would only end up in the shops and I really would like to look at Mr Smallbone's collection.' He turned to the old man. 'If that's all right with you?'

'It is, Mr Bunting. It would be a pleasure. I have all the time in the world. Just let me get the keys and we'll have a good look round. Heaven knows, I have so few visitors nowadays. We can start with the Alvis.'

'Not a TD 21, surely?' Roger asked, wide-mouthed.

'What other Alvis would one have? Come on, follow me.'

'Are you coming Sylvia? You might find it rather interesting for a change,' uttered Roger, arching his eyebrows as if to suggest that it would be advisable to accompany the men.

Sylvia paused for a moment as if to consider the wisdom of an argument. But since his return to work he had been much more assertive, and she knew there were times when he wasn't to be contradicted. His attitude indicated that this was one of them. She kept her mouth shut.

'Of course, darling. I'm sure it will be fascinating.'

Even Sylvia couldn't believe her own eyes. They followed the old man through the back door which opened out on to a tiny expanse of mossy lawn bordered at the rear and sides by a towering bank of leylandii. Let into the right side bank was a small gate, almost hidden by the dense evergreen foliage of the trees. They walked through the gate in single file, Mr Smallbone leading, then Sylvia, finally Roger bringing up the rear. The sight that met them on the other side of the green wall made Sylvia and Roger gasp in amazement.

The expanse of ground that opened out in front of them was huge. It must have been 200 yards long by 100 yards wide at its far end. The trapezium-shaped ground was occupied by three massive wooden barns, one adjacent to each of the trapezium's longer sides, and one nestling against the far, shorter boundary. A green and cream double-decker bus stood in the open space between the barns.

'I haven't yet worked out how I can get it under cover,' rued the old man, scratching his chin with a gnarled and weatherbeaten hand. 'It would cost far too much to build a structure around it. Such a pity as it's one of the few of its kind. I know I should sell it really, but I can't bring myself to do it.'

'What is it?' asked Sylvia, staring at the upper deck of the bus.

'It's a 1939 Cravens RT 1499. Very rare. They've nearly all been broken up. Went out of regular service in 1979. I got this one for next to nothing from the City of London Transport Authority. Worth a fortune now. Had the dickens of a job getting it into the back. Had to hire a driver in the end.'

'It's magnificent,' opined Roger.

As impressive as the double-decker was, it was overshadowed by the sheer scale of the three wooden barns around the perimeter.

'There's a logic to the way I've laid the collection out,' indicated Mr Smallbone. 'We'll start over here. Please follow me, and kindly shut the door behind you.'

Roger and Sylvia couldn't believe what was unfolding before them. In the first of the barns there was a 1937 Austin 10 Cambridge, a 1946 Riley RMA 1.5, a 1954 Riley RME, and a 1960 Ford Zephyr. All were neatly displayed with an information board for each one, describing the type, history and personal provenance. Mr Smallbone was thorough, very thorough.

'The first three of my decades,' remarked Mr Smallbone.

The tour continued through the second barn where the old man continued to fascinate them with his collection of pristine cars from the fifties and sixties.

Finally, they entered the sweep of the last barn. This one was empty, save for the presence of a virginal white Triumph Stag. The group halted in front of the car.

'And this,' said Mr Smallbone indicating with his hand a recently swept space next to the Triumph, 'is where…'

'Dolly,' prompted Sylvia.

'Dolly,' echoed Mr Smallbone, 'will be in residence.'

So here I am, gathering dust with bygone generations for company. In still life, tucked away in a hidden place, out of sight. A reminder of a once-mighty industry now deceased.

The sadness of it all is that nobody cared as it quietly slipped into obscurity. Not the drivers, who wanted better value and quality for their money. Not the assemblers, who didn't give a toss anyway, even though they were throwing away their livelihoods. Not the managers, who were constantly caught in a fog of incompetence. Not even the Government, who had simply had enough and were glad to be shot of the problem.

Not even Roger and Sylvia.

But I do have a gorgeous lady next to me to keep me young.

Postscript: The Code of Conduct

The Code of Conduct is not to be confused with the *Highway Code* that is followed by the drivers. Drivers are nowhere near as intelligent as cars and their Code considers every possible situation a driver may find himself in. Our Code of Conduct is much more based on common sense and an appreciation of what's right and proper.

Rule 1: Secrecy with drivers
Never, ever reveal what sex you are to any driver. Don't even think of doing so. The consequences are too dire to mention.

Rule 2: Behaviour towards female cars
Never, ever, make any kind of improper advances to a car of the female sex. Never try to tailgate, and never park too close. Respect the female car's space and her right to privacy. If she wants to tailgate you, that's her prerogative. Don't complain, it can be quite enjoyable.

Rule 3: Behaviour towards the old
Always, always allow an old car to enter from the side road by indicating with a flash of your headlights. Do not rush the old, they may have lost a lot of the horsepower they once had. Remember, one day you too will be old.

Rule 4: Behaviour towards other parties (original)

4(i)   Don't play games with the bikes. They have been around a lot longer than you have and they'll probably be here when you're long gone.

4(ii)   Don't bully the motorbikes. They may be smaller than you but if they gang up there could be serious trouble.

4(iii)   Don't take on the lorries. You will never, repeat never, win an argument with a lorry.

4(iv)   Don't always do what the drivers want you to do. Experience has proven they are prone to errors of judgement. The consequences could be fatal.

4(v)   Do give clear warning of your intentions to speed up, slow down, turn left, or turn right. The designers have had the good foresight to provide you with lights and indicators specifically for this purpose.

4(vi)   Do defer to the pedestrians. They need to cross the road many times in the course of their everyday lives, and the footpath was invented specifically for them. They are special.

4(vii) Do be cautious of animals that have a strange fascination for the road. Foxes, stoats, weasels, and badgers that dash across, hedgehogs that walk along, rabbits that stop and stare at you, and particularly pheasants, which have a kamikaze commitment to flying in your face at every opportunity.

4(viii) Do be aware of the sharp bends. The road has a tendency to curl like a coiled snake, and like a snake it has the ability to wind and unwind at breakneck speeds.

4(ix)   Do read the signs that the road has put out for you. If the road has requested you to slow down there is a reason for it. The road is not given to frivolity and you will not find sympathy if the signs are ignored.

Rule 4: Behaviour towards other parties (amended)

4(i)   Don't give a shit about the bikes. They're only small and what does it matter if they get knocked about from time to time? Nobody listens to them anyway. They can always use the footpath.

4(ii)   Don't pay any attention to the motorbikes. If they do gang up (which isn't likely nowadays) we can always drive straight through them.

4(iii) Don't worry about the lorries. They're much slower than us now and we can run rings around them. And that can be quite fun.

4(iv)   Do always obey the drivers. They have tremendous power and if they don't like you they'll trade you in. There is no loyalty nowadays.

4(v)   Don't give clear warning of your intentions to speed up, slow down, turn left, or turn right. It's up to the other drivers to anticipate your every move. If they can't, tough for them.

4(vi)   Do try to annoy the pedestrians. It can be tremendously amusing to frustrate them as they try to cross the road. This forces them to use the footpath where they will fight with the bikes.

4(vii) Do try to destroy any animals that have a strange fascination for the road. It's a great game to play. If you're lucky (and accurate) and happen to hit a rabbit or pheasant, the driver will usually stop and quietly slip the (hopefully) dead animal into the boot. They'll make a great meal later. You'll be in his good books for ever.

4(viii) Do try to beat the sharp bends. That's what they're there for isn't it? You know the designers have made you so that you can negotiate them on two wheels if desired.

4(ix)   Do ignore the signs that the road has put out for you. It's about time the road got a sense of humour.

Rule 5: Management of sensitive information
Never reveal secrets to a driver. They will twist what you tell them and use it against you to their advantage and your dismay.

Rule 6: Common courtesy
Always be polite and courteous to other cars. It is this, above all else that distinguishes cars from the drivers.

Printed in Great Britain
by Amazon

51315499R00118